Adam traced his fingers up and down her spine as Melanie leaned into him.

He was drawn back into the memory of having her in his apartment, the way she felt in his arms. Her words from that night came rushing back. *You feel like a dream.*

"I shouldn't have hugged you. It was unprofessional."

"I thought we were taking a break from professional."

She reared her shoulders back and looked him in the eye. "Are you going to let me go?"

"As near as I can tell, you're holding on to me just as tight."

She rolled her eyes—childish from most women, adorable from Melanie. "I'm trying to keep myself upright."

He was certain he'd heard every word she'd said, but her lips were so tempting and pouty that it was hard to grasp details. "Then stop being upright."

Before Melanie knew what was happening, Adam was kissing her. And like a fool, she kissed him right back.

Dear Reader,

Thanks for picking up my debut for Harlequin Desire!

Over the course of writing *That Night with the CEO*, I became very attached to my characters. Adam Langford is smooth, out-of-bounds smart and he delivers a sexy line like none other. I'd also describe him as stuck—between his own business empire and the one his father wants him to run, between his ladies' man reputation and his deep desire to find the one woman who understands him.

That's where our heroine, public relations whiz Melanie Costello, comes in. I adore Melanie. I want to drink beer and watch college basketball with her. Melanie is a fighter. Dumped by her fiancé, facing career challenges galore, she still persists.

Another character deserving a mention is Adam's dog, Jack. He was inspired by a mastiff/Great Dane mix by the same name. Jack was owned by dear friends who invited my family and me to stay in their home after we had a devastating house fire. Jack was my savior. He followed me everywhere, waited for me when I went to bed, always with his head on my pillow. I love animals and have always had pets, but I'm not sure I've ever had a bond with an animal like the one I had with Jack. My sweet doggie boyfriend departed this earth a few years ago. I'll always miss him.

I love to chat with readers, so feel free to send me an email at karen@karenbooth.net anytime.

Thank you so much for reading!

Karen

THAT NIGHT
WITH THE CEO

—

KAREN BOOTH

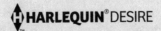 HARLEQUIN® DESIRE

Recycling programs
for this product may
not exist in your area.

ISBN-13: 978-0-373-73407-8

That Night with the CEO

Copyright © 2015 by Karen Booth

Printed in U.S.A.

www.Harlequin.com

Karen Booth is a Midwestern girl transplanted in the South, raised on '80s music, Judy Blume and the films of John Hughes. She loves to write big-city love stories. When she takes a break from the art of romance, she's teaching her kids about good music, honing her Southern cooking skills or sweet-talking her supersupportive husband into mixing up a cocktail. You can learn more about Karen at karenbooth.net.

Books by Karen Booth

Harlequin Desire

That Night with the CEO

Visit the Author Profile page
at Harlequin.com or karenbooth.net.

For Bobbi Ruggiero and Patience Bloom. We share an unbreakable bond—the sisterhood that comes from loving John Taylor for more than thirty years. Now, let's arm wrestle for him.

One

Women had done some nutty things to get to Adam Langford, but Melanie Costello was going for a world record. Adam watched on the security camera as her car pulled through the gate in the most relentless rain he'd seen in the four years since he'd purchased his mountain estate. "I'll be damned," he mumbled, shaking his head.

Thunder boomed.

His dog, Jack, nudged his hand, whimpering.

"I know, buddy. Only a crazy person would drive up here in this weather."

The hair on his arms stood up, but the electricity in the air wasn't from thunderstorms. The anticipation of seeing Melanie for the second time in his life left him off-kilter. She'd done a number on him a year ago, giving him the most consuming night of passion he could remember and then slipping out the door before he awoke. There'd been no goodbye whispered into his ear, no nudge to wake him for a parting kiss. All she'd left behind was a memory he couldn't shake and countless questions, the most pressing of which was whether she'd ever make him feel that alive again.

He hadn't even known her last name until a week ago, not that he hadn't tried like hell to figure it out after she disappeared. No, it had taken a personal nightmare of monstrous proportions—a tabloid scandal that refused to die—to bring Melanie Costello to him. Now she was here to save his ass from the gossip rags, even though he doubted anyone could do that. If any other public relations person had been given this job, he would've found a way out of it, but this was his chance to capture lightning in a bottle. He had no intention of passing that up, even if he also had no intention of letting the lightning know that he remembered her. He wanted to hear her say it. Then he would get his answers.

The doorbell rang and Adam made his way over to the fireplace, jabbing at the smoldering logs. He stood before the flames, staring into them as he polished off his small-batch bourbon. He was needled by guilt, knowing Melanie was standing outside, but she could wait to begin the reformation of his public image. She'd been in such a hurry to leave him alone in his bed. She could sit tight for a few minutes before he'd let her in.

It was just Melanie Costello's luck that she'd end up regretting the best sex of her life. As recently as a week ago, her one night with Adam Langford was her delicious secret, a tingly memory that made her chest flutter whenever she thought about it, and she thought about it a lot. The phone call from Adam's father, Roger—the call that required a confidentiality agreement before they could speak a single word—had put an end to that. Now the flutter in her chest had sunk to her stomach and felt more like an elbow to the ribs.

Melanie parked her rental car in the circular driveway of Adam Langford's sprawling mountain retreat. Tucked away on a huge parcel of land atop a mountain outside Asheville, North Carolina, the rustic manor, complete with tall-peaked roofs and redwood arches, was lit up in spectacular fashion against the darkening night sky. She couldn't have been any more impressed or intimidated.

Cold smacked her in the face as she wrestled her umbrella, her pumps skating over the flagstone driveway. *I'm the only woman boneheaded enough to wear four-inch heels in a monsoon.* She bound her black raincoat against her body, shuffling to a grand sweep of stone stairs. Icy raindrops pelted her feet, the wind whipped, her cheeks burned. Lightning crackled across the sky. The storm was far worse now than it'd been when she'd left the airport, but the most daunting assignment of her public relations career, retooling Adam Langford's public image, required prompt attention.

She scaled the staircase, gripping the rail, juggling her purse and a tote bag weighed down with books on corporate image. She eyed the door expectantly. Surely someone would rush to usher her inside, away from the cold and rain. Someone had opened the gate. Someone had to be waiting.

No welcoming party appeared at the towering wood door, so she rang the bell. Every passing second felt like an eternity as her feet turned to blocks of ice and the cold seeped through her coat. *Don't shiver.* Once she caught a chill, it took her forever to warm up. Imagining the man waiting for her, Adam Langford himself, only made her more certain she'd never stop trembling if she started.

Memories flashed, of one glass of champagne, then two, while watching Adam across a crowded suite at The Park Hotel on Madison Avenue. Perfectly unshaven, he wore a slim-cut gray suit that flaunted his trim physique so well that it had made her want to forget every etiquette lesson she'd ever learned. The party had been the hottest invitation in New York, held to celebrate the launch of Adam's latest venture, AdLab, a software developer. Prodigy, genius, visionary—Adam had been given countless labels since he earned his fortune with the headline-grabbing sale of social media website ChatterBack, all before he graduated summa cum laude from Harvard Business School. Melanie had snagged an invitation hoping to network with potential clients. Instead, she did the last thing she'd ever imagined, going home with the man of the hour, who had one more notable label on his résumé: notorious philanderer.

He'd been so smooth with his approach, building heat with eye contact as he wound his way through the bustling room. By the time he'd reached her, the notion of introductions seemed absurd. Everyone in the room knew who he was. Melanie was a virtual nobody in comparison, so he'd asked for her name, and she'd answered that it was Mel. Nobody called her Mel.

He'd held on to her hand when he shook it, commenting that she was the highlight of the party. She blushed and was immediately sucked into the vortex of Adam Langford, a place where sexy glances and clever quips reigned supreme. The next thing she knew, they were in the back of his limo headed to his penthouse apartment while his hand artfully slid beneath the hem of her dress and his lips roamed the landscape of her neck.

Now that she would again be in the presence of the man who'd electrified her from her pedicure to her last hair follicle, a man from a powerful Manhattan family and who had no lack of money or good looks or mental acumen, she couldn't help but feel queasy. If Adam recognized her, the "absolute discretion" his father had demanded would fly right out the window. There was nothing discreet about having slept with the man whose bad-boy public image she'd been hired to overhaul. Adam's reputation for one-night stands had certainly contributed to the wildfire nature of the tabloid scandal. She shuddered at the thought. Adam was her only one-night stand, ever.

It seemed rude to ring the bell a second time, but she was freezing her butt off. The sooner she and Adam got the first chunk of work done tonight, the sooner she could be in her pj's, warm and toasty under the comforter at her hotel. She pressed the button again, just as the latch clicked.

Adam Langford opened the door, wearing a navy and white plaid shirt, sleeves rolled to the elbows, showing off his muscled forearms. Jeans completed his look, an appealing contrast to the suit she'd last seen him wear. "Ms. Costello, I presume? I'm shocked you made it. Did you pick up a canoe at the airport?" He held the door with one hand while the other raked through his thick chestnut-brown hair.

She laughed nervously. "I upgraded to the fan boat."

Melanie's heart was a jackrabbit thumping against her chest. Adam's steely-blue eyes, edged with absurdly dark lashes, made her feel so exposed, naked. She knew full well that other aspects of his manner could make her feel the same way.

He smirked, welcoming her inside with a nod. "I'm sorry if you had to wait. I had to put my dog in the other room. He'll charge at you if he doesn't know you."

She averted her gaze. There was no way she'd sustain another direct hit from his eyes so soon. She held out her hand to shake his, which was impossibly warm. "Mr. Langford. Nice to see you." She'd stopped short of saying "*meet* you," since that would've been a big fat lie. When she'd accepted this job, she'd rationalized that Adam kept company with countless women. How could he possibly remember all of them? Plus, she'd lopped off her hair and gone from dishwater blond to golden since their tryst.

"Please, call me Adam." He shut the door, mercifully cutting off the cold. "Did you have any problems finding the place in the rain?"

He'd greeted her with the niceties you reserve for a stranger, and for the first time since he'd opened the door, she felt as though it was okay to breathe. *He doesn't remember me.* Perhaps it was okay to make eye contact again. "Oh, no. No problem at all." The complexity in his eyes held her frozen, stuck in the memory of what it had felt like the first time he looked at her, when he seemed to be saying that she was all he wanted. Those eyes were enough to leave her tongue-tied. "Piece of cake." Apparently they also made her want to lie, as she'd just spent two hours squinting through a foggy windshield and cursing the GPS.

"Please, let me take your coat."

"Oh, yes. Thank you." This wasn't what she'd expected. Adam Langford had enough money to hire an assistant for someone to take her coat. She fumbled with the buttons and turned herself out of it. "No hired help up here in the mountains?"

He hung her coat in a closet and she took that millisecond to smooth her black dress pants and retuck her gray silk blouse. After the long, stressful drive from the airport, she had to be a wreck.

"I have a housekeeper and a cook, but I sent them home hours ago. I wouldn't want them out on the roads."

"I know I'm a few hours late, but we really need to stay on schedule. If we can go over the media plan tonight, we can devote the entire day tomorrow to interview preparation." She reached into her bag and removed the books she'd brought.

He blew out a deep breath and took them, examining

the spines. "*Crafting Your Image in the Corporate World*? You can't be serious. People read this?"

"It's a fabulous book."

"Sounds like a real page-turner." He shook his head. "Let's take this into the living room. I could use a drink."

Adam led her down a far-reaching hall and into a cathedral-like great room with redwood-beamed ceilings. A sprawling sectional and leather chairs made an inviting seating area, softly lit by a dimmed wrought iron chandelier and a blazing fire. Floor-to-ceiling windows spanned the far wall, animated by raindrops pattering the panes against the backdrop of the gray evening sky.

"Your house is stunning. I can see why you'd come here to get away."

"I love New York, but you can't beat the quiet and the mountain air. It's one of the only places I can take a break from work." Adam rubbed his neck, stretching the shirt taut across his athletic chest, showing her a peek of dark chest hair her fingers had once been wonderfully tangled in. "Although apparently, work somehow managed to find me."

Melanie forced a smile. "Don't think of it as work. We're fixing a problem."

"I don't want to insult your profession, but isn't it tiring spending your day worrying about what other people think? Molding public opinion? I'm not sure why you bother. The media says whatever they want to. They couldn't care less about the truth."

"I think of it as fighting fire with fire." She knew that Adam would be a difficult case. He hated the press, which made the persistent nature of what was now known as the Party Princess scandal much worse.

"Frankly, the whole thing seems like a colossal waste of money, and I can only assume that my father is paying you a lot of it."

But you wouldn't want to insult my profession. She pursed her lips. "Your father is paying me well. That should tell you how important this is to him." As annoyed as she was by Adam's diatribe, the retainer from his father was greater than she'd make from her other clients combined this month. Costello Public Relations was growing, but as Adam had alluded to, it was a business built on appearances. That meant a posh office space and an impeccable wardrobe, which did not come cheap.

A bark came from the far side of the kitchen, the door beyond the Sub-Zero fridge.

Adam glanced over his shoulder. "Are you okay with dogs? I put him in the mudroom, but he'd really rather be where the action is."

"Oh, sure." She nodded, placing her things on a side table. "What's your dog's name?" She already knew the answer, and that Adam's dog was a sweet two-hundred-pound hulk—a Mastiff and Great Dane mix.

"His name is Jack. I'll warn you. He's intimidating, but he'll be fine once he gets used to you. The first meeting is always the roughest."

Jack yelped again. Adam opened the door. The dog barreled past him, skidding on the hardwood floors, taking the turn for the great room. Jack thundered toward Melanie.

"Jack! No!" Adam may have yelled at the dog, but he made no other attempt to stop him.

Jack sat back on his haunches and slid into her. Immediately, Melanie had a cold dog nose rooting around in the palm of her hand. Jack whacked his sizable tail against her thigh.

She hadn't bargained on Adam's dog ratting her out by revealing that they shared a past, too. "He's friendly."

Adam narrowed his stare. "That's so strange. He's never done that with anyone he's never met. Ever."

Melanie shrugged, averting her eyes and scratching

behind Jack's ears. "Maybe he senses that I'm a dog person." *Or maybe Jack and I hung out in your kitchen before I left your apartment in the middle of the night.*

The only sound Melanie could hear were Jack's heavy breaths as Adam stepped closer, clearly appraising her. It made her so nervous, she had to say something. "We should get started. It'll probably take me a while to get back to my hotel."

"I'm still not sure how you got up the mountain, but you aren't getting back down it anytime soon." He nodded toward the great room windows. It was raining sideways. "There have been reports of flash floods in the foothills."

"I'm a good driver. It'll be fine." She really was nothing more than a skittish driver. Living in New York meant taxis and town cars. She kept her license valid only for business trips.

"No car can handle a flood. I have room for you to stay. I insist."

Staying was the problem. Every moment she and Adam spent together was another chance for him to remember her, and then she'd have a lot of explaining to do. This might not be a great idea, but she didn't have much choice. She wouldn't get any work done if she was lost at sea. "That would give me one less thing to worry about. Thank you."

"I'll show you to one of the guest rooms."

"I'd prefer we just get to work. Then I can turn in early and we can get a fresh start in the morning." She took a pair of binders from her bag. "Do you have an office where we can work?"

"I was thinking the kitchen. I'll open a bottle of wine. We might as well enjoy ourselves." He strode around the kitchen island and removed wineglasses from the cabinet below.

Melanie lugged her materials to the marble center

island, taking a seat on one of the tall upholstered bar stools. "I shouldn't, but thank you." She flipped open the binders and slid one in front of the seat next to hers.

"You're missing out. Chianti from a small winery in Tuscany. You can't get this wine anywhere except maybe in the winemaker's living room." He cranked on the bottle opener.

Melanie closed her eyes and prayed for strength. Drinking wine with Adam had once led down a road she couldn't revisit. "I'll have a taste." She stopped him at half a glass. "Thank you. That's perfect." The first sip took the edge off, spreading warmth throughout her body—an ill-advised reaction, given her drinking buddy.

Jack wandered by and stopped next to her, plopping his enormous head down on her lap.

No. No. You don't like me. Melanie squirmed, hoping to discourage Jack. No such luck.

Adam set down his glass, his eyebrows drawing together. "I swear, Miss Costello. Something about you is so familiar."

Two

"People say that I have a familiar face." Melanie's voice held a nervous squeak. She turned and practically buried her face in her project binder.

Adam considered himself an expert at deciphering the underlying message in a woman's words, but he was especially fluent in coy deflection. *I can't believe she's going to try to hide this.* "Have you done any work for me?"

She shrugged and scanned her blessed notebook. "I would've remembered that."

Time to turn up the heat. "Have we dated?"

She hesitated. "No. We haven't dated."

To be fair, she might have him on a technicality there. They hadn't *really* been on a date. He scoured his brain for another leading question. "Do I detect an accent?" A slight twang had colored the word *dated*.

She screwed up her lips and sat straighter, still refusing to make eye contact, which was a real shame. Her crystalline blue eyes were lovely—plus, he'd be able to tell if she was being deceitful. "I grew up in Virginia."

"I met a woman from Virginia at a party once. She was a real firecracker. Maybe a little bit crazy. If only I could remember what her name was." He rubbed his chin, took another sip of wine, rounding to the other side of the kitchen island and taking the seat next to hers. Jack hadn't moved, standing sentry at her hip. *That's right, buddy. You know her.*

"I'm sure it's difficult to keep track of all of the people you meet." She pointed to a page titled "Schedule" in his notebook. "So, the interviews…"

He scanned the page, getting lost in a confusion of publication names and details. "No wonder my assistant was panicked this afternoon." He flipped through the pages. "I generally work eighteen-hour days. When exactly am I supposed to find time for this?"

"Your assistant said she'll rearrange your schedule. Most interviews and photo shoots will take place at your home or office. I'll do everything I can to make sure your needs are met."

Right now, his greatest need was to seek comfort in a second bourbon as soon as he'd dispatched the Chianti. Continuing this charade held zero appeal, and her refusal to own up to their past was frustrating as hell. He needed the question that had been hanging over his head for the past year to be answered. How could a woman share an extraordinary night of passion with him and then disappear? Even more important, *why* would she do that?

"For the moment, the biggest interview is with *Metropolitan Style* magazine," she continued. "They're doing a feature on you and your home, so that will entail a photo shoot. I'm bringing in a professional home stager to make sure that the decor is picture-perfect. Jack will need to see a groomer before then, but I'll take care of that."

Adam bristled at the idea of home stagers messing with his apartment, but no one decided what happened with his dog. "Jack hates groomers. You have to hire my guy, and he's always booked weeks out." Of course, his groomer would make himself available whenever Adam needed him, but it was the principle.

"I'll do my best, but if he isn't available, I'll have to hire someone. Jack is important. People love dogs. It will cast you in a more favorable light."

"How did you know I have a dog anyway?"

She cleared her throat. "I asked your assistant."

She had a roundabout answer for everything. He'd never endure an entire weekend of talking in circles. "What if I didn't already have a dog? What would you do then? Rent one?"

"I do whatever is needed to make my clients look good."

"But it's all a lie. Lies catch up with you eventually."

Dropping her pen down onto the notebook, Melanie took a deep breath. She rolled up the sleeves of her silky blouse with a determination that made him wonder if she wanted to flatten him.

"The home stager is a waste of time," he added. "My apartment is perfect."

"We need it to look like a *home* in the photographs, not a bachelor pad."

He saw his chance. She knew what his apartment looked like, but only because he'd seduced her in it. "So I have to get rid of my neon beer sign collection? Those things are everywhere." He hadn't owned one of those since college, but he wouldn't hesitate to fabricate absurdities to get her to spill it.

She twisted her lips. "We can work around that."

He had to up the bachelor-pad ante. "Now, what about the stuffed moose head above the mantel? Does that scream single guy or does that just say that I'm manly?" That was hardly his taste either, and she knew it.

"I don't know." She rubbed her temple. "This isn't really my area of expertise. Can we come back to this later?" Melanie clenched a fist, waves of frustration radiating from her.

"No. I want to get this straightened out now." His mind raced. His goal in sight, he was prepared to crank out crazy ideas for hours. "There are the beer taps in the kitchen, and I need to know if they'll photograph my bedroom. I have a round bed, like in James Bond movies."

"That's ridiculous."

"Why? Lots of men have moose heads and James Bond beds."

"But you don't," she blurted.

The color drained from her face, but that gorgeous mouth of hers was just as rosy pink as he'd remembered. Just thinking about her lips traveling down the centerline of his chest charged every atom in his body. She didn't say another thing, but he swore he could hear her heartbeat, drumming between her heavy breaths.

"How would you know?" he asked, wishing he felt more triumphant at having caught her.

She straightened in her seat, struggling to compose herself. "Uh…"

"I'm waiting."

"Waiting for what, exactly?"

"Waiting to hear the real reason why you know I have a dog and what my apartment looks like. I'm waiting for you to just say it, *Mel*."

Melanie's shoulders drooped under the burden of her own idiocy. Her mother had always been emphatic that a lady never lies. Melanie had already skirted the truth, and she didn't want to be that person. "You remember me."

"Of course I do. Did you honestly think that I wouldn't?"

His disbelief made her want to shrink into nothingness. How could she have been so foolish? "Considering your reputation with women, I figured I was a blip on the map."

"I never forget a woman."

His response might have prompted extreme skepticism if he hadn't said it with such conviction. He hadn't forgotten her. She knew for a fact that she hadn't forgotten him. Of course, there were probably lots of other women he hadn't forgotten, too.

"You changed your hair," he said.

Her pulse chose a tempo like free-form jazz—stopping and starting. He really did notice everything. "Yes, I cut it."

"The color's different. See, I still remember what it looked like splayed across the pillows of my bed." He rose from his seat and stalked back around the kitchen island, refilling his wineglass. Plainly still angry, he didn't offer her more. "Did you really not see a problem with taking this job even though we'd slept together? I'm assuming you didn't reveal that little tidbit to my father. Because if you had, he never would've hired you."

Adam was absolutely right. She'd stepped into a gray area a mile wide, but she needed the payday that came with this job. Her former business partner had crippled her company by leaving and sticking her with an astronomical office lease. The crushing part was that he'd also been her boyfriend—nearly her fiancé—and he'd left because he'd fallen in love with one of their clients.

"I would hope we could be discreet about this. I think it's best if we just acknowledge that it was a one-time thing, keep it between us, and not allow it to affect our working relationship." Mustering a rational string of words calmed her ragged nerves, but only a bit.

"One-time thing? Is that what that was? Because you don't seem like a woman who runs around Manhattan picking up men she doesn't know. Trust me, I meet those women all the time."

Did it bother him that it had been a one-night stand? She wasn't proud of the fact either, but she never imagined it would even faze Adam. "I didn't mean to say it like that."

"What about the contract my father had you sign? The clause about no fraternization between you and the client?"

"Exactly why I thought it best to ignore our past. I need this job and you need to clean up your image. It's a win-win."

"So you need the job. This is about money."

"Yes. I need it. Your father is a very powerful man, and having a recommendation from him could do big things for my company." Why she'd put her entire hand out on the table for him to see was beyond her, but she wasn't going to sugarcoat anything.

"What if I told you that I don't want to do this?"

She swallowed, hard. Adam was doing nothing more than setting up roadblocks, and they were becoming formidable. If he wanted to, he could end her job right then and there, send her packing. All she could do now was make her case. "Look, I understand that you're mad. The scandal is horrible and I didn't make things any better by hoping that you wouldn't recognize me. That was stupid on my part, and I'm sorry. But if you're looking for a reason to go through with this, you don't need to look any further than your dad. He's not just worried about his company and your family's reputation. He's worried about what this will do to your career. He doesn't want your talents to be overshadowed by tabloid stories."

Dead quiet settled on the room. Adam seemed deep in reflection. "I appreciate the apology."

"Thank you for accepting it." Had she finally laid this to rest? She took a deep breath and hoped so.

"And yes, it was incredibly stupid on your part. I'd go so far as to call it harebrained."

There went the instant of newfound calm, just as Melanie's stomach growled so loudly that Adam's eyes grew as large as dinner plates.

"Excuse me," she mumbled, horrified, wrapping one arm around her midsection to muffle the sound.

"Coming up with bad ideas must've made you very hungry."

"Very funny. I'm fine." She shifted in her seat, mad at herself for not owning up to the fact that she would've killed for a day-old doughnut. Her stomach chimed in, as well.

"I can't listen to that anymore," he declared. "It's unsettling." He marched to the fridge and opened it, pulling out a covered glass bowl. "My cook made marinara before I sent her home. It'll take a few minutes to make pasta."

"Let me help." Desperate for the distraction of a new topic, she shot out of her bar stool and walked to the other side of the island. Jack followed in her wake.

"Help with what? Boiling water?" He cast her an incredulous smirk. "Sit."

"Are you talking to me or Jack?"

He cracked half a smile and she felt a little as if *she* might crack. In half. "You. Jack can do whatever he wants."

"Of course." She filed back to her seat and watched as he filled a tall pot with water and placed it on the six-burner cooktop. "Careful or I might have to book you an appearance on the Food Network."

"You should see me make breakfast." He sprinkled salt into the water then placed a saucepan on the stove and lit the flame beneath it. "I could've made you my world-famous scrambled eggs if you hadn't done your Cinderella routine that night and taken off."

The man had no fear of uncomfortable subjects. What was she supposed to say to that?

"Care to comment, Cinderella?"

"I'm sorry." She cleared her throat and picked at her fingernail. "I couldn't stay."

Adam spooned the sauce into the pan, shaking his head. "That's a horrible excuse."

Excuse or not, there was no way she could've stayed. She couldn't bear the rejection of Adam running her off the next morning. She couldn't bear to hear that he'd call her when she knew that he wouldn't. She'd already suffered one soul-crushing brush-off that month, from the guy she'd thought she would marry. The pain of a second would've prompted the question of whether she might make a good nun. "I'm sorry, but it's the truth."

Wisps of steam rose from the pot, and the aroma of tomato sauce filled the air. Adam dropped in a package of fresh pasta and gave it a stir. "All I'm wondering is why you wouldn't stick around when you have that kind of chemistry with someone. At least say goodbye or leave a note. I didn't even know your last name."

When he had the nerve to say it out loud—to be so rational about it—it sounded as if she'd done the most insane thing ever. *Wait. Chemistry?* She'd assumed that what she'd felt was mostly one-sided, a lethal combination of champagne and Mr. Smooth. Regret and embarrassment weighed on her equally. What if she'd stuck around? Would he have said what he was saying now? "Hopefully you can find a way to forgive me."

He narrowed his gaze, eyes locking on hers. "Maybe someday you'll tell me the real reason."

Oh, no, that's not going to happen.

The timer buzzed. Adam gripped the pot handles with a kitchen towel and emptied the contents into the prep sink. Steam rushed up around his face and he blew a strand of hair from his forehead. He slung the towel over his shoulder, capable as could be, adding the noodles to the sauté pan and giving the mixture a toss with a flick of his wrist. The most brilliant man to hit the business world in recent history, the man who'd given her the most exhilarating night of her life, was toiling away in the kitchen. For her.

Adam divided the pasta into two bowls and grated fresh Parmesan on top. He set one bowl before her and filled her wineglass then topped off his own. Tempting smells wafted to her nose, relief from her epic hunger in reach. He took his seat, saddling her with a return of nerves. Now that they were shoulder to shoulder again, she was acutely aware of the specter of Adam Langford.

"Cheers," he said in a tone still more annoyed than cheery. He extended his arm and clinked her glass with his.

"Thank you. This looks incredible." She took a bite. It was far better than her usual Friday night fare, Chinese takeout on the couch. She dabbed at her mouth with the napkin. "This is delicious. Thank you." Quieting her rumbling stomach was wonderful, but they hadn't resolved the greater issue—she still wasn't sure he was willing to let her do her job. "Now that we've talked through things, are we okay to get to work tomorrow? We need to bury the Party Princess scandal."

"Can we put a ban on saying that? No man wants a scandal, but the princess part just makes it worse."

"I know it's awful. That's precisely why I'm here. I can make all of that go away."

"I don't see why we can't just ignore it. Aren't we feeding the fire if we go on the defensive?"

"If we had a year or more, that might work, but with your father's illness, there just isn't that kind of time. I'm so sorry to say that. I really wish that part was for a different reason."

"So you know. The timetable." Adam blew out a deep breath and set down his fork.

Her heart went out to him. She could only imagine what he was going through, about to ascend to the immensely powerful job he'd likely dreamed of since he was a boy, all because his father's cancer was terminal. "Yes. He told me in confidence. I think he needed me to understand just how urgent this is. It's crucial that the board of directors see you in a better light so they'll approve your appointment to CEO. The scandal needs to be a distant memory by the time the succession is formally announced at the company gala. That's only a few weeks away."

"The board of directors. Good luck with that." He shook his head, just as his phone rang. "I'm sorry. I have to take this."

"Of course."

Adam got up from his seat and walked into the living room. Melanie was thankful for a break from persuading him that she could do this. Even if he cooperated, the pressure of turning around public perception in a month was monumental. She wasn't entirely sure she could pull it off. She only knew that she had to.

"I'm so sorry," he said, when he got off the phone. "Problems with the launch of a new app next week."

"Please don't apologize. I understand." Melanie got up and took her dish to the sink. She rinsed it and put it in the dishwasher. "You should finish your dinner. I'm going to grab my suitcase and get some rest. If you could point me in the direction of the guest room."

"Call me old-fashioned, but no woman should have to go out in the rain for a suitcase. I'll do it." He held up a finger, just as she was about to protest. "I insist."

She watched from the doorway as he braved the rain and wind without a jacket. His hair and shirt were soaked by the time he was back inside. He stomped on the entryway rug and combed his fingers through his dripping-wet hair. Her mind flashed to their night together—stepping out of the shower with him, sinking into the softest bath-mat she'd ever felt beneath her feet. He'd raked his hand through his soaked locks, a sultry look in his eyes that said he was ready to claim her again. He'd coiled his arms around her naked waist, pressed his hands into her back, and kissed her neck so delicately that she'd trembled be-neath his touch.

She might faint if she ever saw him toy with his wet hair again.

"Your room is upstairs. Second door on the right."

Adam trailed behind her as she climbed the grand stair-case.

"This one?" she asked, poking her head inside, still a bit light-headed from the memory of the shower.

Adam reached past her and flipped on the light, illumi-nating a bedroom outfitted with a beautifully dressed king bed, a stacked stone fireplace and its own seating area. "I hope this will work." He followed her into the room, placing her suitcase on a luggage stand next to a gorgeous Craftsman-style bureau.

"It's perfect." Melanie turned to face him, his physical presence exercising undue influence on her as he rubbed the closely cropped stubble dotting his jawline. Her brain wasn't sure how to react to his kindness, but her body knew exactly what it thought. The flutter in her chest returned. Heat flooded her, the memory of his fingers tracing the length of her spine while he had her in a bed much like the one she was standing next to. "Thank you for everything. The room. Fetching my suitcase."

"I hate to disappoint you, but I'm not the cad the world thinks I am." He strode past her, stopping in the doorway.

She wasn't sure what Adam was, where exactly the truth lay. Maybe she'd find out this weekend. And maybe she'd never know. "That's good. That will make it a lot easier to show the world the best side of Adam Langford."

A clever smirk crossed his face. "You've seen me naked, so I'd say you're definitely qualified to say which is my best side."

Melanie's brain sputtered. Her cheeks flamed with heat.

"Good night," he said, turning and walking away.

Three

Melanie sat up in bed, half-awake, tugging the butter-soft duvet to her chest. Last night hadn't gone according to plan, but in many ways, it was a relief to have the whole, stupid, ridiculously hot thing out in the open.

It'd taken hours to fall asleep. Adam's reminder that she'd seen him naked had only set her on the course of determining which side was indeed his best. After revisiting their night together…kissing in the limo, unzipping her dress in his living room, peeling the paint off the walls in the shower…she'd decided the front. Definitely the front.

Too bad she could never see him like that again.

She threw back the covers and glanced outside at the open vista of the grounds surrounding the house. A creek rushed along the edge of manicured gardens, threatening to breach its rocky banks. Towering pines framed the view of the Blue Ridge Mountains beyond. It was a new day, storms a distant memory. Time to start fresh.

She retrieved her makeup bag, beelining to the beau-

tifully appointed guest bath—gray granite countertops
and silvery glass tile, a soaking tub for two. After a quick
shower, she dabbed on foundation and undereye concealer
to hide her lack of sleep. A sweep of blush, some eyeliner
and a coat of mascara came next. Polished was appropri-
ate, not done-up.

Finishing with a sheer layer of pale peach lip gloss,
Melanie rubbed her lips together and popped them to the
mirror. She could hear her mother's syrupy Virginia drawl.
You catch more flies with honey than vinegar. She remembered first hearing that when she was a little girl, only
six years old. It was the strongest memory she had of her
mother, which also made it the most bittersweet. She and
her sisters lost her to a car accident months later.

Melanie ruffled her pixie-cut hair and swept it to the
side. Lopping off and dying her hair to exorcise the memory of her lying, cheating ex might have been drastic, but
she'd had this crazy idea about renewal. It hadn't really
worked. She still hadn't gotten past the fact that she'd
thought Josh would propose. She hadn't forgotten that
he'd packed up and left with another woman, leaving her
to fend for herself. No, she might've looked a little different on the outside, but she was the same Melanie on the
inside—hurt some of the time, lonely most of the time,
determined not to quit all of the time.

Back in her room, she slipped on a white scoop-neck
tee, black cardigan and slim-fitting pair of jeans. She
stepped into ballet flats and hurried downstairs, the smell
of coffee wafting in from the kitchen. She was invigorated,
undaunted, ready to go. And then she saw Adam.

You've got to be kidding me. She'd come downstairs
prepared to work, but she hadn't bargained on Adam's
bare chest. Or his bare stomach. Or an extra eight hours
of scruff along his jaw and the narrow trail of hair below

his belly button. More than that, she hadn't bargained on any part of him glistening with sweat.

"Morning." He stood in the kitchen, consulting his phone. "I made coffee. Let me get you a mug." He turned, opened the cabinet and reached for a coffee cup. Gentlemanly behavior, all while showing off the sculpted contours of his shoulders and defined ripples of his back.

Her eyes drifted south, calling into question whether the front really was the best. The way he filled out the rear view of his basketball shorts made a compelling case for the back. Then she remembered what that view looked like without clothes. She was all kinds of conflicted over the best-side verdict.

"Cream? Sugar?" he asked, filling her mug.

"Both, please." She shook her head in an attempt to think straight. "I'll do it."

"Help yourself." He gestured to a small white pitcher and sugar bowl. "Sleep well?"

She spooned the sugar into the mug, gluing her focus to the steaming coffee. "I did, thank you. I'm ready to get started whenever you are. We have a lot of ground to cover today."

"Already got in my workout."

"So I see." She turned, but even a fraction of a second was too long to look at Adam right now. Her eyes darted all over the room, desperate for something undesirable to look at.

"Is something wrong?"

"No. It's just…" Her voice trailed off, betraying her. "You can't put on a shirt?"

"Why? Does it bother you? I can't help the fact that I'm hot." He grabbed her attention with his blazing smile, smoothing his hand over the flat plane of his stomach.

"Excuse me?"

"Hot, as in temperature hot."

Damn him. "It's a little difficult for us to keep things professional when you're traipsing around the house half-dressed."

"I assure you, I have never once traipsed."

"Regardless, isn't it polite to wear a shirt to breakfast?"

"It is. My mother always made me wear one when I was a kid. She also told me to floss every day and wear clean underwear. So I'll be two-for-three today. Nobody's perfect."

He knows what he's doing. He's making me crazy because he can. "Look, we have a ton of work to do. I suggest you grab a shower so we can start."

"It'll go faster if I have someone to scrub my back."

"Adam, please. The contract I signed? No fraternization or interpersonal relations? I take those things very seriously, and I know your dad does, too."

"We both know the only way to enforce that is the honor system." His eyebrows bounced.

"Yeah, well, you need to keep your honor system in your pants."

"Hey, you're the one suggesting showers. Not me."

Melanie exhaled in exasperation. "Things will go smoother today if you cooperate. Why do you have to joke around about everything?"

"Because it's Saturday and I work my ass off all week and I'd much rather read a book or catch a game on TV than practice answers to interview questions and talk about whether or not you think Oprah will like me."

"First off, Oprah said no. Secondly, I know you hate this, but we have to put the scandal to an end." Her phone buzzed. "Excuse me. I should check this." She reached into her pocket. The push notification on her phone did not bring good news. "There's something new in the papers this morning. A reporter got your ex-fiancée to comment on the scandal." She shook her head, feeling a little sorry for Adam. "This is why you need to let me do my job. This can't be what you want."

Adam buried his face in his hand. Jack wandered over and nudged Adam's hip. "Hey, buddy." Adam's voice was tinged in sadness, which seemed odd considering his fondness for his dog. He crouched down and looked Jack in the face, ruffling his ears. "No, that's not what I want."

Adam parked himself on the long leather bench in his walk-in closet and untied his sneakers, cradling his cell phone between his ear and shoulder. His mother answered after a few rings.

"Mom, hi. Is Dad around?"

"Well, hello to you, too. You don't want to talk to me?"

"Of course I want to talk to you, but I was hoping to talk to Dad and see how he's doing." He peeled off his socks and tossed them across the room, connecting with the hamper.

"Your father's fine. I'm screening his calls. Otherwise, he takes work calls all weekend and never gets any rest. He needs his rest."

Dad. Once a workaholic, always a workaholic. "Has he been tired since he got home last night?"

"Yes. Fridays are the worst. I don't know why he continues with this charade of going into LangTel every day."

"I don't know why he does it either."

LangTel was the telecom corporation Adam's father started from the ground up in the seventies. Adam had grown up heir apparent, but once he went to Harvard Business School, he realized that—just like his father and every Langford man before him—he would never be content taking over someone else's empire. He wanted to build his own, which was precisely why he started his first company while he was still in school. It made him his first fortune before the age of twenty-four.

Even so, when his parents had asked him to help run LangTel from behind the scenes after his father first fell ill, he had done his familial duty. At the time, Roger Langford's prognosis was uncertain and they didn't want him to appear "weak" for fear of the company stock plummeting.

It was meant to be a dry run and Adam passed with flying colors, but it was the worst year of his life—preparing to launch his current company while running interference at LangTel. The timing couldn't have been any worse—right on the heels of his fiancée ending their two-year relationship. LangTel had worn a hole in his psyche.

"At some point," Adam continued, "we're going to have to tell the world that his cancer is far worse than anyone realizes. I'm tired of the song and dance."

"I agree, but your father doesn't want to say a word until things have been cleared up for you with, you know, the newspapers."

His mother couldn't bring herself to utter the word *scandal*, and he was thankful for it. At least it had been only photographs that had been leaked and not something worse, like a sex tape. Adam glanced at his Tag Heuer watch, which sat atop the mahogany bureau in the center of the closet. It was nearly nine thirty and Melanie had been clear that she was ready to get to work. "Hey, Mom. Can I put you on speaker?"

"You know I hate that."

"I'm sorry. I just have to get into the shower in a minute." He pressed the speaker icon on his iPhone. He shucked his basketball shorts and boxer briefs and tossed them over his head, but missed the hamper this time. "I'll talk to Dad about it when I'm back in the city. Maybe I can come by on Sunday afternoon after I fly in."

"Be sure you call first. There are still photographers camped outside our building. You might have to sneak in through the service entrance."

Such a pain. It was one thing for him to have to deal with the photographers, quite another for his mother and father to have to do it. "Okay." He grabbed his robe from the end of the bench and slipped it on.

"If you want to stay for dinner, we could invite your sister, too. Your father and I would love that."

"That sounds great. Anna and I can work on Dad, see if we can talk to him some more about working Anna into the succession plan for LangTel. We both know she'll do an incredible job." He no longer talked to his parents about the fact that he didn't want to run LangTel. It was always dismissed as ludicrous. Now his focus was getting his dad to give his sister, Anna, the chance she wanted and deserved.

"Your father would never dream of letting your sister run the company. He wants Anna shopping for a husband, not sitting in a boardroom."

"Why can't she do both?"

"I'm about to lose your father, and now you don't want me to have any grandchildren? You won't have any until you find the right woman, and Lord knows when that will happen."

There she goes. "Look, Mom. I have to go. I have a houseguest and I need to shower." He strode into the bathroom, across the slate tile floor.

"Houseguest?"

He reached into the shower, cranking the faucet handle. "Yes. Melanie Costello, the woman Dad hired to do this futile PR campaign."

"It's not futile. We need to preserve your father's legacy. When he's gone, you'll be the head of this family. It's important that you're seen for your talents, not for the women you run around with."

He sighed. He didn't like that his mom saw him this way, but he also didn't like feeling as if he couldn't make his own damn decisions, bad or not. He'd be thirty-one soon, for God's sake.

"So tell me. Is she pretty?" she asked.

He couldn't help but laugh. "Mom, this isn't a date. It's work. Nothing else." He couldn't tell his mother that he wouldn't mind if this was a date or that he and Melanie had a past. He certainly couldn't tell her how much he loved being around Melanie, even when she got mad. It made her already vibrant blue eyes blaze, which was particularly intoxicating when packaged with gentle curves and those unforgettable lips.

The mirrors in the bathroom began to fog up. "I need to go, Mom. Tell Dad to call me if he has a chance. I'm worried about him."

"I'm worried, too, darling."

Adam said his goodbyes and slid his phone onto the marble vanity. He dropped the robe to the floor and stepped into the spray, willing the hot water to wash away his worry about his father, if only for a moment. His mother wasn't doing well either. He could hear the stress in every word she said.

He lathered shampoo and rinsed it away. However heartbreaking his father's illness, he could do nothing about it except to make his father's final months happy ones. That was much of the reason Adam had agreed to the PR campaign. The final deciding factor he'd kept to himself—the instant he looked up the Costello Public Relations website and saw Melanie's picture, he had to say yes. After a year of wondering who she was, he not only knew the identity of his Cinderella, he'd be working with her.

Adam shut off the water and toweled himself dry before heading back into his walk-in closet, bypassing the custom-made suit he'd worn on the corporate jet into Asheville. Those clothes were made for the city, and he relished a respite from Manhattan and the media microscope. He certainly preferred the uniform of his freer existence in North Carolina—jeans, plaid shirts and work boots. Choosing to dress in exactly that, he headed downstairs to find Melanie, curious how she planned to air his dirty laundry in public.

Four

The inside of Melanie's purse might have resembled a yard sale, but she never forgot where she put something.

"Have you seen my binders? The ones with the interview schedule?" she asked, peeking behind the cushions of the massive sectional in Adam's living room. Nothing.

Adam was tending the fire, a welcome sight even though the rain had cleared up. "Not the binders again. Can't you send that to me in an email? I'll read it off my phone." He stood and brushed the legs of his perfect-fitting jeans. She had a weakness for a man in an impeccably tailored suit, but a close second was a guy dressed exactly as Adam was. Each held its own appeal—in-command businessman and laid-back mountain guy. So of course Adam had to knock both looks out of the park.

"I like paper. I can rely on paper," Melanie said as she headed into the kitchen and tapped the counter. "It's so weird. Did I bring them up to my room?" She went for the stairs, but didn't make it far. Her notebooks sat mangled behind one of the leather club chairs. She scooped them up. "Did you feed these to Jack?"

Adam was tapping away on his phone. "What? No. Did you actually leave those out where he could get them?"

"I assumed they'd be safe on the coffee table."

"Um, no. He's only three. As well trained as he is, he might as well be a puppy. He'll chew on anything if you give him the chance."

She flipped through the notebooks. One had massive teeth holes at the corners, and the binding of the other was twisted. "I hope he enjoyed his snack."

Jack was sound asleep in front of the fire.

"I'd say he's dead-tired after it."

"We should probably concentrate on interview preparation anyway. You're going to need coaching."

"You can't be serious. I'm unflappable." He sat on the couch, running his hand through his touchable head of hair, giving off a waft of his cologne or shampoo or perhaps it was just plain old Adam. Regardless, it made Melanie's head do figure eights.

"Okay then, Mr. Unflappable." She took a seat opposite him. "We'll do a mock interview and see how you do."

"Fine. Good."

Melanie clicked her pen furiously, well acquainted with the techniques writers might use to put Adam on edge. "Mr. Langford, tell me about that night in February with Portia Winfield."

Adam smiled as if they were playing a game. "Okay. I went out, I ran into Portia. We'd met a few months ago at a party. We had a few too many drinks."

"Don't say how much you had to drink. It casts you in an unflattering light."

"Why? It's a free country."

"Never, ever say that it's a free country. It's an excuse to do whatever you want, without regard for the consequences." She ignored the scowl on his face. "Now try again. Tell me about that night in February."

There was deep confusion in Adam's expression. Hopefully that meant he was realizing what a narrow tightrope he had to walk to get past a scandal. "That question is so open-ended, and I already told you the truth. Now I don't even know where to start."

"These journalists are skilled in the art of tripping someone up. They want you to say something embarrassing or break down. They want something juicy. It's your job to control the conversation. Make the scandal exactly what you claim it to be."

"Which is?"

"You tell me." She flipped her pen in her hand, watching him. The gears were turning behind his dappled blue eyes. For someone with an IQ that was reportedly off the charts, this was clearly a puzzle to him.

"I didn't go to the club with her. I just ran into her."

"That makes it sound like you were there to pick up women. Focus on the benign or the positive. Nothing that can be construed as negative."

He pressed his lips together in a thin line. "I'd been working like crazy on a new project and I wanted to blow off some steam."

"I'm sorry, but that won't work either. The work stuff is good, but blowing off steam makes you sound like a man who uses alcohol to have fun."

"Well, of course I do. What's the point, otherwise?" He sank back against the cushions. "You know, I don't think I can do this. My brain doesn't work like this. People ask me a question, I answer it and move on."

"I know this is difficult, but you'll get it. I promise. It's just going to take some honing of your answers."

"Why don't you show me what you mean? If I don't defer to you on this, we'll be sitting here for days."

"Okay. First off, you establish your relationship with Ms. Winfield. Maybe something like, 'I've known Portia Winfield for a few months and we're friends. She's a delightful woman, a great conversationalist.'"

He cocked an eyebrow and smirked. "You do know she's not the sharpest tool in the shed, right?"

"All I said is that she's amusing and can talk a lot."

A flicker of appreciation crossed his face. "Go on."

Melanie deliberated over what to say next, not enjoying the idea of Adam with another woman. Feeling that way was irrational. She had no claim on him, and Adam's reputation suggested that he could have any woman he wanted. Just last year he had a brief romance with actress Julia Keys, right after she'd been deemed the most beautiful woman in the world. Melanie remembered well standing in line at the drugstore, seeing Julia's perfect face on the cover of that magazine, a distinct sense of envy cropping up, knowing that Julia was dating the man Melanie could have for only one night.

"You could say that you two enjoyed a drink together," Melanie said, collecting her thoughts.

"It was more like three and she was well on her way when I got there."

"But it's true that at some point in the evening you enjoyed one drink, right?"

"Sure."

"There you go."

He grinned. "Please. Keep going."

"Here's where I get stuck, because I can't figure out exactly how you two ended up kissing, while the back of her dress was stuck in the waistband of her panties, the famous disappearing panties."

Adam sighed and shook his head in dismay. "Do you have any idea how idiotic this whole story is?"

"You're going to have to paint me a picture, because I really don't."

Adam folded his arms across his chest. "I kissed her, and it was more than a peck on the mouth. That much is true. But I quickly realized how drunk she was. I wasn't about to let it go any further. I had no idea she was mooning half of the bar. She'd just come back from the ladies' room. And I definitely didn't know that anyone was taking pictures with a camera phone."

As the woman who had more than once tucked her skirt into her pantyhose by accident, Melanie knew this was a plausible explanation. "Then what?" Curiosity overtook her, even when the story was making her a bit queasy.

"I told her that I thought it would be a good idea for me to walk her to her car so her driver could take her home. I settled up the tab while she went back to the ladies' room. I walked her outside, but she could hardly walk and was hanging on me. She dropped her phone on the sidewalk, bent over to pick it up, but I still had my arm around her. That's when she showed the entire world her, well, you know..."

"Ah, yes. The hoo-ha that launched a million internet jokes."

"I'm telling you, I had no idea."

"And from that, the world assumes you took her panties off at the bar."

"Of course they do, but that's not what happened. I have no idea what she did with them or why she took them off in the first place. I was trying to be a good guy."

"The reality is that the press loves to catch famous people doing stupid things, but the bad publicity doesn't hurt her like it hurts you. All she does is ride around in a limo all day and go shopping. If anything, this probably makes her more interesting to her fans."

"I never should've bought her a drink. Or kissed her for that matter."

She almost felt sorry for him. He hadn't done anything wrong. It had all gone horribly awry.

"Are you going to tell me what my ex said in the paper about the scandal? I don't think I can read it for myself."

Melanie cringed, knowing how bad it was. If her ex had ever said anything this ugly about her, she'd probably curl into a ball and die. "I don't think we should worry about that. Nothing good will come from it. As far as the PR campaign goes, we're going to have to hope that today was just a slow news day."

"No. I want to know. Tell me." He spoke with clear determination.

"Just remember. You asked." Melanie pulled the article up on her phone, sucking in a deep breath. "She said, and I quote, 'I'd love to say that this surprises me, but it doesn't. Adam has always had a huge weakness for pretty girls. I don't know if Adam is capable of taking any woman seriously. I certainly don't think he's capable of love. I feel sorry for him. I hope someday he can figure out how to be with a woman and finally give of himself.'"

Adam shot up from the couch, marched over to the fireplace and began anxiously jabbing the logs.

"I know you're mad, but setting the house on fire won't solve anything," she said.

"Do you have any idea how hurtful that is? I'm not capable of love? She was my fiancée. We were going to get married and have kids."

Call it an occupational hazard, but Melanie often had to look past clients' hurt feelings over the way they'd been treated by the media. It was far more difficult in Adam's case, because she'd experienced the same rejection. She knew how hard it was to go on, alone, living a life that bore no resemblance to the one you'd thought you'd have.

No wedding bells, no home to make together, no children to love and care for.

"You obviously loved her very much."

"I did. Past tense." He returned to poking at the fire. "The minute she walked out on me, I knew she never really loved me."

Melanie had to wonder if that was true, if he'd known right away that it hadn't really been love. It'd taken her months to figure that out when Josh left, and in many ways, that made the pain far worse. "Why did she break it off? If you don't mind me asking." Her curiosity was too great not to ask.

"She said I was too wrapped up in work." He shrugged and left the fire to blaze away. "If you ask me, I think she was disappointed I didn't want to feed off the Langford family fortune and jet around the world, going to parties. It's ridiculous. I work hard because that's the way I'm built. I don't know any other way."

"There's no shame in working hard."

"Of course not, but I don't get to tell my side of the breakup in the papers. I just have to accept the awful things she said about me."

"I'm sorry. I know it's difficult to have your personal life on display like this."

"I'm not the guy in those pictures. You do realize that, don't you?"

"Unfortunately, that's all people care about."

Adam shook his head in disgust. "The whole thing is so ridiculous. Can't we go back to my plan? Ignoring it?"

"Not if you want Portia Winfield's lady parts to be the first thing people think of when they hear your name."

He groaned and plopped down on the couch again. "Let's keep going."

Melanie closed her notebook and set it on the coffee table. She needed to switch gears for both of their sakes.

"Let's discuss wardrobe. For most of these photo shoots, I'd like you to appear polished, but still casual. We'll do a suit for the business publications, but for the lifestyle magazines, I'm thinking dark jeans and a dress shirt. No tie. I'd love to see you in a lavender shirt. It will bring out your eyes, and women react well to a man who isn't afraid to wear a softer color."

"You have got to be kidding. I wear blue, gray and black. I wouldn't know lavender if it walked up to me and started talking."

"I'm not asking you to pick the color out of a box of crayons. I'm asking you to wear it."

"No lavender. No way."

Melanie pressed her lips together. There were only so many battles she could win. "We'll do blue. A light blue. Nothing too dark. You'll have to wear makeup too, especially for the TV appearances, but you don't need to do anything other than sit there and let them take care of it. It's painless."

"How'd you learn all of this, anyway?"

"Public relations? I studied it in college."

"No. The things about lavender and women liking softer colors."

"Let's just say I grew up in a family that cared a lot about appearances." That may have been underselling it a bit, but she wasn't eager to open up this particular can of worms.

"Oh, yeah? Like what?"

She dismissed it with a wave of her hand. "Trust me, it's boring."

"Look, I need a mental health break after the mock interview and the quote from the paper. Just tell me."

She didn't want to dismiss him, mostly because she hated it when he did the same to her. Maybe the highlights, or lowlights as she referred to them, would be okay.

"Both of my parents were big on appearances, although my mother passed away when I was little, so I don't remember being lectured about it by her." The way Melanie missed her mom wasn't what she imagined to be normal. She'd been so young when she lost her, that it was more like losing a ghost than a real person. "I definitely remember it from my dad."

Adam frowned. "Like what?"

Melanie shrugged, looking down into her lap. She'd told herself many times that she shouldn't allow these memories to make her feel small, but they did. "He'd order me to put on a dress, or try harder with my hair, be more like my sisters. I'm the youngest of four girls and I was a little bookish growing up. They were all into beauty pageants. My mother had won tons of pageants as a girl, but she was stunning. I knew I'd never live up to that."

"Why? You're pretty enough."

She blushed. It was silly, but she enjoyed hearing Adam say she was pretty, or at least pretty enough. "There's more to it than that. You have to walk up on stage and smile perfectly and wave your hand a certain way and follow a million rules that somebody, somewhere, decided were the ways a girl should present herself. I couldn't do it. I couldn't be that plastic girl."

He rubbed the stubble along his jaw. "And yet you chose a profession that involves an awful lot of smoke and mirrors."

She'd never really thought of it that way. "But I can make my own rules when I need to, make my own way. It's creative and strategic. I love that part of my job. It's never dull."

"Did you participate in any beauty pageants, or did you rebel from the beginning?"

A wave of embarrassment hit her, quite a different type of blush from the one she got when Adam had said nice things. "I did one pageant. I actually won it, but that was enough for me."

"Little Miss Virginia? You're from Virginia, right?"

"Yes. Rural Virginia. The mountains. And I can't tell you what my title was or I'll have to kill you. It's far too humiliating."

"Well, now you *have* to tell me. No one gets past me without sharing at least one humiliating story."

She shook her head. "Nope. Sorry. We're discussing business. Let's get back to your wardrobe."

"Come on. We already had to talk about me and the girl who can't keep track of her own undies. And one could argue that this is business. These are your qualifications for being my wardrobe consultant."

"It's dumb."

"What if I say I'll wear a lavender shirt? One time." He held up a single finger for emphasis.

She really did want him to wear lavender. It would make for some great pictures. "Okay. Fine. I was crowned Little Miss Buttermilk. I was five."

Adam snickered. "I can't believe you won the coveted Little Miss Buttermilk title."

Melanie leaned forward and swatted him on the knee. She'd never told any man this stupid, stupid story, not even her ex. "If you must know, I think I largely took it based on the talent portion. I was an excellent tap dancer."

"I have no doubts about that. I've seen your legs, Buttermilk."

Melanie swallowed, hard, and tucked one leg under the other. Had he ever seen her legs—every last inch of them. Adam cleared his throat. Thankfully, Jack got up from his nap and ambled over, providing a logical means of changing the topic.

"Hey, buddy." Adam scratched Jack behind the ears.

"Your parents must've made you do things you didn't want to do when you were a kid."

"It's always been about business. Some kids got baseball mitts for Christmas from their dad. I got a briefcase." Adam nodded, looking at Jack. "That actually happened, by the way. No lie. I love my dad, though. I really do." That sadness was in his voice again, the one that cropped up whenever he spoke of his father.

"That's why you agreed to let me come. To make your dad happy."

His eyes connected with hers, holding steady for a few, insanely intense moments. "That's a big part of the reason. Of course."

Five

Adam's brain was mush. There was no more gas in the tank. He and Melanie had talked about interviews and wardrobe for hours. They'd delved into the details of his past that they needed to focus on, and the ones they absolutely needed to avoid. She'd lectured him about refraining from flipping the bird to the photographers when they got pushy. He'd done it only once, but he still wasn't sure he could make any promises on that last point.

He rolled his neck, admiring Melanie as she eyed her watch for what had to be the third or fourth time. She was especially lovely in the fading light of day, with a golden pink flush to her cheeks that closely matched the lips he'd never be able to forget. "Do you have somewhere you need to be, Buttermilk?"

"Hey. Are you really going to call me that? Because I kind of hate it."

"Really? Because I kind of love it." It wasn't the nickname that he loved. It was her reaction, the way she got a little riled up but still seemed to enjoy some part of it.

"If you're going to call me that, then at least turn on the TV so we can watch some basketball. My team is playing." She smiled as if she couldn't keep it inside any longer. "Actually, it's our league championship. This is the first year in a really long time that we've been any good."

"Yeah. Of course." He picked up the remote and turned on the TV. "But wait. The NBA championship isn't until June."

"I'm talking college." She shook her head and cast him a glance over her shoulder, a glance that stopped him dead in his tracks. Those blue eyes of hers were magic. Flat-out magic. "March Madness, baby."

He couldn't have fought a smile if he'd wanted to. He loved hearing her say "baby," especially coupled with a sports reference. It was the sexiest damned thing ever. "Your wish is my command." He scanned through the channels until he found her game. "I'm more of an NBA guy than college, but I'm up for anything."

She scooted to the edge of her seat, watching the screen intently as a pair of announcers pontificated about the game, dozens of screaming fans camera-hogging behind them. "The college game is so much better than the pros." She didn't tear her eyes from the TV. "I can't stand to watch a game with a bunch of millionaires standing around, not playing defense."

"Sounds like most of the parties I go to."

"I bet."

He'd hoped he'd get a laugh out of that one, but this seemed to be serious business for Melanie.

"Do you have any beer?" She granted him another glance, smiling sheepishly. "Just seems like we should be drinking beer if we're going to watch this. Plus, I need to take the edge off. If we lose, I might die."

Adam hopped off the couch. "Beer coming up. Stat." He strode into the kitchen, took two beers from the fridge, popped the tops off, grabbed a bag of potato chips from the pantry and returned to the living room.

"Thank you." She gazed up at him, their fingers touching as she took the bottle. Her eyes were as wide as they were deep—he could spend a lifetime unraveling everything behind them. She waved him out of the way, craning her neck. "Can you move? I can't see. It's time for tip-off."

He obliged her request and settled near her, leaving a polite distance, wishing they could sit hip to hip. If he didn't think she'd slug him in the stomach, he would've leaned back with his arm across the back of the couch, hoping she'd settle in and rest her head against his shoulder. What would it be like to have a night with Melanie again? To have her curl into him, kiss him, trail her fingers along his jaw. It was painful to imagine, and yet he didn't want to ignore the visions that ran through his head.

When Melanie had come through his door twenty-four hours ago, he wasn't sure exactly what he'd expected, although he knew what he'd hoped. He'd longed to hear her confess that leaving him in the middle of the night was the most stupid, rash decision she'd ever made, that she hoped he could forgive her, that she wanted a second chance.

She hadn't come close to giving him that. If he were being impartial, he understood her reasons, however disappointing. So instead of another searing-hot liaison, he got to watch basketball and drink beer with her, a woman who was smart and determined and so effortlessly sexy. It could've been worse.

She might've expected that he'd watch the game, too, but he couldn't pass up the chance to study her. It was much like the first time he'd seen her, at the party at The Park Hotel. He'd noticed her because she'd been talking to one of his biggest business rivals. Her musical laugh filtered through the crowded space, rose above the din of chatter, spiking his curiosity. As he trudged his way through dry conversations about investors and start-ups, he struggled to keep his eyes off her. Her entire being came alive when she spoke. She was a beacon in a sea of dullness. Every phony, contrived exchange he'd had that night had left him starved for something real. He hadn't quite bargained on how real their night together would be, or how much it would disappoint him when she left.

He quickly learned that he could read everything happening in the game from her actions. If her team was shooting free throws, her hands flew to her temples, fingers crossed. If they made a fast break, she launched herself off the couch and yelled, "Go! Go!" If the other team had the ball, she groaned, "Guard him!" and "Get the rebound!" ESPN had nothing on Melanie Costello in terms of sports entertainment.

Ninety minutes later, after the roller coaster of Melanie's jubilation and dismay, her team was down by one point, with twelve seconds left. Her resignation was plain during the commercial break. "I should've known it was too good to be true." She turned to him, her long bangs falling across her forehead, making her look so sweet, so vulnerable. "We always find some way to choke."

The disappointment in her voice was almost too much for him to take. If she were his, he wouldn't have hesitated to pull her into a snug embrace. Hell, he would've paid off a referee or two if it meant her team could win and she'd be happy. "You never know. Plenty of time to get off a good shot."

"Yeah, right. That's never going to happen."

The station cut away from commercial back to the game. The announcers speculated as a player for Melanie's team waited to throw the ball inbounds.

Melanie again sprang up from the couch. "I can't even

look." She bounced up and down on her toes, shook her hands at her side as if they'd gone numb. Adam had to admire the appealing shape of her rear view, especially as she nervously wiggled in place. He longed to have his hands on that part of her again, caressing her soft skin, pulling her closer.

The announcer spoke. *Miller inbounds the ball, full-court pass to Williams down in the key. He's double-teamed. Nowhere to go.*

"Oh, no," Melanie blurted.

He kicks it back out to Miller. He hasn't hit a shot all night.

"Just shoot it!" Melanie screamed.

He steps back behind the three-point line. The shot is off. We have the buzzer...and it's good!

Melanie whipped around, her eyes like saucers. "It's good!" She charged at him with open arms, flattening him against the back of the couch. "Oh my God, Adam. We won," she said breathlessly. "You were right." She trembled with excitement.

He reflexively wrapped his arms around her, breathed in the sweet smell of her hair. "So I heard. It's wonderful." *But not as wonderful as this.*

"I'm sorry." She distanced herself a few inches, shaking her head. Now that she was there, he wasn't about to let her go without at least a moment of discussion. "We haven't won the championship since I was a kid."

"Don't be sorry. This is the highlight of my entire weekend." He traced his fingers up and down her spine as she leaned into him, both of them still sitting, but definitely leaning. He was drawn back into the memory of having her in his apartment, the way she felt in his arms, as if these limbs of his were made for nothing other than keeping her close. Her words from that night came rushing back. *You feel like a dream.*

"I shouldn't have hugged you. It was unprofessional."

"I thought we were taking a break from professional."

She reared her shoulders back and looked him in the eye. "Are you going to let me go?"

"As near as I can tell, you're holding on to me just as tight."

She rolled her eyes—childish from most women, adorable from Melanie. "I'm trying to keep myself upright."

He was certain he'd heard every word she'd said, but her lips were so tempting and pouty that it was hard to grasp details. Mostly he wanted this to keep going. "Then stop being upright."

Before Melanie knew what was happening, Adam was kissing her. And like a fool, she kissed him right back.

Melanie had all kinds of resolve until the kiss. Good God… His mouth and hands and his broad, taut frame. He was temptation, served up on a silver platter. He was the fuel to her fire—bodies pressed together, her body weight against his, her lips absolutely starved for more. The fire inside her finally had what it had waited to feed on.

His lips were impossibly gentle, even when there was no mistaking his powerfully male intentions. He wanted her. He was in charge. She felt it in every grasp as his hands slipped under her sweater, cradling her waist, his strong arms effortlessly rolling her to her back. He kissed her cheek, trailing to her jaw and the delicate spot beneath her ear—the spot that made electricity zip along her spine. She arched into him, eyes closed, mind floating in the nether, between the present and her past.

The night she shared with Adam hadn't been a dream. She hadn't built it up in her head—kissing him really was unlike kissing any other man. Sublime, a never-ending moment of pleasure to sink into. He was real. This kiss was real. Perfect. She hadn't spent the past year aimless. She'd spent the past year missing this kiss.

His leg pressed between hers, white-hot friction in just the right place. Adam was the last man to touch her there, to fill her every need. He was the last man she'd wanted like this. It was almost too perfect. Could they start where they left off? Forget the past year? Erase it?

"I've wanted to do this since you walked in the door last night," he mumbled, unbuttoning her blouse. "The minute I saw you again, I had to have you."

She drank in his wonderfully possessive words, his strong hand gliding across her stomach. She had to have him, too. They were on the same page, except he seemed to be reading ahead—everything he did was exactly what she was hoping for. He trailed his finger along the lacy edge of her bra, ever so slightly dipping it beneath the fabric, bringing her skin to life.

But her brain barged into the conversation. *What in the hell are you doing? You can't do this. You need this job. Didn't you spend the past year vowing to never allow a man the chance to destroy your heart and your career in one fell swoop?*

Her body warred with the logic. *But I want him. I've waited a year for him. Nobody would ever have to know.*

But you would know.

Adam's hand was on her back, at her bra strap. *Pop.*

Oh, no. "Adam. Stop. We can't." She expected him to groan in frustration, possibly even push her back in disgust, but he didn't.

"Are you okay? What's wrong?" He cupped the side of her face, washing his thumb over the swell of her cheek.

"I'm sorry. I'm so sorry, but we can't. We can't do this." She shut her eyes, needing a break from the allure of his mouth, especially when his breath was brushing her lips. She had to collect her thoughts. "I never should've let it go this far. It's just that…" She stopped herself. The more she explained, the stupider she would sound. And eventually she would have to admit that if she had her way, if her job didn't mean everything and if she could suspend belief and think for a second that Adam would want her for more than a fling, they'd be upstairs in his bed right now. They would be making memories that put the first night they shared to shame.

"It's just what?" he asked. "Did I do something wrong?"

How could he still be so calm? She was about to frustrate the hell out of him. Surely he had to realize what was happening. She felt him against her leg, hard and ready, and yet he was worried that he'd done something wrong. "I'm sorry. It's just not right."

"I don't understand. Do you have a boyfriend? Because I never would've made a move if I'd known that."

"No, I don't have a boyfriend. This is just wrong. I signed a contract. It would be a mistake."

"A mistake." Adam sat up, distancing himself from her, creating a cold and uncrossable divide. Maybe that was for the best, although it didn't feel like the best. It felt awful. "You really have a way with words when you aren't concerned with the public relations spin, don't you?"

His question left her thinking that he had a way with words as well—his cut her to the core, not so much with *what* he said, but with the way he said it. With little effort, he left her feeling hollowed out. And that put her on the defensive. "I thought you deserved the truth."

"I'm not really sure what I deserve, but right now it feels like I'm being punished for something I can't help."

She got up from the couch, buttoning her blouse. She couldn't believe he was going to use *that* as his excuse. "I'm very sorry about that." She pointed in the general direction of his crotch. "A cold shower might help."

"Cute. Real cute. That's not what I mean."

"Oh. Sorry." Wave after wave of embarrassment battered her. Could she possibly make this any worse? She didn't dare try to make it better. "Look, I'm sorry. I think we should just say good-night and forget this ever happened."

He shook his head, not looking at her. "Whatever you say."

She thought she'd felt hollowed out before, but now it was as if she didn't exist. Wanting to do nothing but hide, she rushed upstairs and closed the guest room door behind her, ducking under the comforter and curling into a ball. Tears came, and she hated that more than anything.

How was she going to do this job? How would this ever work? She couldn't spend day after day coaching Adam through interviews and running interference at photo shoots. She'd never make it, knowing how badly she wanted him, knowing what a horrible idea it was to give in to feelings like that.

She wiped her cheeks, willing the tears to stop. She had to get through this or else she'd fail, and that couldn't happen. She just had to get her act together and find a way to get Adam off her mind. She needed a plan.

Six

Before last night, when was the last time Adam had been turned down? He didn't care to remember, but it sure stung. The fact that it came from Melanie and that he'd waited an entire year for a chance only made it worse. Was he really that far off base about their chemistry? Because she certainly seemed to care a hell of a lot more about her job than about him.

When she pressed against him on the couch, he'd had only one thought—the electricity was back. It jolted every atom of his body. How could that be one-sided? How could two people create that much heat if only one person felt it? How else could she so easily put on the brakes? Something didn't add up, that was for sure.

Melanie clopped down the stairs with her overnight bag in tow. He wished he hadn't noticed how pretty she was in the morning, fresh-faced and lovely, even when wearing a distinct frown.

"I would've gotten that for you if you'd asked," he said, pulling his jacket out of the closet.

"I'm okay to do it myself."

"I'm sure you are." He folded his arms across his chest. Creating a physical barrier made it easier to ignore his deep desire to invite her back upstairs and kiss her as he had last night, only this time with an entirely different, naked, ending.

She drew a deep breath in through her nose, avoiding anything beyond a blip of eye contact. "I need to ask a favor. I just got a notification from the airline that my flight is overbooked. They bumped me."

"And?" He had a strong suspicion about the question that was coming. He just wanted to hear her ask for it.

"I was wondering if there's room on your corporate jet for me to ride along."

"I don't know. Jack really prefers having two seats. He's a big boy."

Melanie dropped her chin, delivering that hot look of admonishment. "Really? Are you really that mad about last night? Because you know as well as I do that it's not a good idea for anything to happen between us. It would be reckless and stupid. It would be a huge mistake."

Adam hadn't planned on prompting that little rant. And would she stop using that damn word—*mistake*? *Well, then.* "Yes, you may join me on the plane back to New York. Of course."

"Oh. Okay. Thank you."

"You're welcome, Buttermilk."

"Did you really just call me that again?"

"It seemed to fit today. Not sure why."

An hour and a half later, they were on board the plane, just the two of them, the pilot and, of course, Jack. Normally, Jack would curl up on the floor at Adam's feet. Sometimes, he'd attempt to climb into his own seat, although that always ended disastrously as he was far too big. Today, he'd parked himself next to Melanie, his head on her lap. *Traitor.*

"Adam, I need to talk to you about something."

Stinging words lingered on Adam's lips. *Oh, really? Something about how you're glad things didn't go any further last night? How we need to remain professional?* "I'm listening." He thumbed through an email on his phone.

"I was thinking that women seem to be your problem, but they could also be your salvation."

"In light of what happened last night, I'd love to know where this is going."

"I thought we agreed we weren't going to talk about last night."

"I didn't agree to anything."

Melanie shook her head as if she couldn't possibly be more frustrated. "One thing I've learned in public relations is that if people have been inundated with a bad image, you can replace it with a more positive image, until eventually they forget the bad."

He looked up from his phone and narrowed his focus. "Like what? Pictures of me volunteering in a soup kitchen? Loading sandbags in a hurricane?"

"No. I was thinking something extremely believable. You. With a woman. Right now, the world thinks you're only capable of meaningless flings, which is the image your parents and the board of directors have such a hard time with."

Adam coughed. If he'd wanted to, he could've gone for the jugular and reminded her that their acquaintance had started out as a one-night stand. As much as the events of last night had scarred his ego, he couldn't do it. He'd never thought of her as a meaningless fling, not even when they'd had only a few hours together. "You want me to start dating classier women."

"Woman. Singular. Basically, you need a girlfriend. A serious one. You need to find a woman and be seen around town together. Ideally, for the next few weeks leading up to the LangTel gala. Then you take her to the party that night, your father makes his announcement about the succession plan, you'll have been in magazines and on talk shows by then. It'll be the unveiling of a brand-new Adam Langford."

He grumbled under his breath. "Great. My debutante ball."

"You know what I mean."

"You're going to find me a new girlfriend?"

"You're going to have to do that part. I do have some criteria for you, though."

Adam slid his phone onto the table next to him and took a sip of club soda, but it felt more like bourbon o'clock. "Can't wait to hear this."

Melanie cleared her throat. "She should be beautiful, of course. You're Adam Langford. No one will believe you're with anyone who isn't stunning."

Jack looked up into her eyes, shot a glance at Adam, and went back to being as close to a lapdog as he could, draping his head across her legs.

"She should be someone who is well-known," Melanie continued. "But she should have a pristine reputation. No more party girls. It should probably be someone who's accustomed to the media microscope. You know as well as anyone how tough that can be to deal with."

"And what do I do with this person?"

"Go out to dinner. Go out for coffee. Take Jack for a walk. You'll just need to let me know ahead of time, so I can leak information to the press."

"I really don't think this is going to work. I'm not good at faking anything. The photographers will see right through it if it isn't real."

Melanie considered him with those blue eyes of hers, the ones he wished he could see looking up at him while she was pinned beneath his body weight, at his mercy. "You might have to get good at faking it."

That was never going to happen. It was already too much work to sit here and talk about another woman. "What happens if I fall in love? After all, I'm hopelessly single and, despite what you might think of me, I don't plan to be that way forever." *Shut up already.*

"Whatever the emotional entanglements are, that's for you to decide."

"Of course." Was this her way of getting rid of him? Pushing him into another woman's arms? If so, she might live to regret it, although he couldn't fathom anyone capturing his imagination the way she had. Perhaps if she were a tinge jealous, it might be enough to make her rethink the wisdom of turning him down.

"Do you have anyone in mind?" Her voice squeaked at the end, as if she'd forced disinterest in the answer.

"I do, actually. I think I know the perfect woman."

The perfect woman. *Great. I can't wait for the perfect woman.*

On paper, Adam finding a fake girlfriend was a beautiful idea, crafted in the middle of the night amid crying jags and brainstorms. It accomplished two very important things—it rounded out Melanie's PR plan, and it created distance between her and Adam. They would be working together a lot. At least if he had to keep his hands to himself, she could do her job and ignore how badly she longed to put her hands all over him.

She glanced at Adam as they rode in his limo on their way back into the city. Her thoughts drifted to what this moment would be like if she and Adam were a couple, if they'd just spent an impossibly romantic weekend at his mountain estate. Surely they'd spent hours making love, hardly ever getting out of bed, except perhaps to tiptoe downstairs for a bite to eat. They'd curled up in front of the fireplace, drifted off to sleep in each other's arms. *Perfect* wouldn't begin to describe it, but *perfect* wasn't reality.

Adam had been on the phone with his father since they landed, discussing LangTel business. She had her own phone call scheduled with Roger Langford tomorrow morning. Would he actually ask her questions about whether or not anything had happened between her and Adam? And what would she say if he did? She'd crossed the line, big-time.

The embarrassment of the scene on the couch Saturday night still ate at her. How could she have gotten so wrapped up in Adam that she hadn't even cared that he'd unbuttoned her blouse? If anything, she'd welcomed it. How could one man have that much influence over her, mind and body? Not even her ex could make her cast aside restraint like that.

Adam said goodbye to his dad and began scrolling through the contacts on his phone. "I was thinking I should get the ball rolling with my new girlfriend. No time like the present."

"Fake girlfriend."

"I told you that I'm not good at faking things. I have to buy into it a little bit or it won't work."

She choked back a sigh of frustration. "Whatever you need to do."

"Just remember," he said, cocking an eyebrow, "it's your fault if I fall in love."

Melanie longed to slap him silly. *Fall in love.* Wouldn't that be the ultimate way for him to get even with her? After all, she hadn't merely left his apartment in the middle of the night. Now she was guilty of losing her moral compass and leaving him with what she'd witnessed as an extra-snug fit in his pants. "As long as you're taking my directives, that's all I care about."

"Here she is." He tapped his phone decisively. "Lovely Julia."

Melanie's stomach turned so sour it was as if she'd downed a gallon of lemon juice. *Julia? Julia Keys?* Was Adam really going to pick an ex-girlfriend and one of the most beautiful women in the history of mankind to be his new fake, but possibly real, girlfriend?

"Julia. It's Adam. How are you, beautiful?"

Beautiful? Melanie sighed. She probably deserved the punishment of listening to this conversation. Desperate for a distraction, she yanked a magazine from her tote bag and began flipping through the pages, imagining they were Adam's very slappable face.

"I hear you're back in New York. I'm hoping we can get together. I have a proposition for you." He leaned back, caressing the black leather seat with his hand.

Was that Julia's effect on him? That merely talking to her made him want to rub things?

"I was hoping I could ask you in person," he said in a voice entirely too sexy for Melanie's liking. "Let's just say that I might have a new role for you. It would involve us spending a lot of time together." He smiled at whatever she said in response.

Melanie pursed her lips, reminding herself that he was doing exactly what she'd asked him to do. *Exactly.* So why was she so pissed off? Oh, right. Because she'd hoped Adam would pick someone pretty and proper and not much else. She certainly hadn't bargained on him picking a woman who exemplified the feminine ideal, nor did she think he would pick someone he might actually fall in love with.

"Would dinner Tuesday night work?" he asked. "I'll have my cook prepare a meal at my place, just so we can talk privately. If you're up for my plan, we can go out for dinner later in the week if your schedule allows." This time, Adam laughed—he practically guffawed—at whatever Julia had said.

Great. She's beautiful, talented, wife material and apparently hilarious. Melanie glared out the window. They were only a block or so from her Gramercy apartment, thank goodness. The end, in sight. She couldn't live through another minute of Adam's phone call. She shoved the magazine in her bag and leaned forward to speak to the driver. "It's right here, on the left."

"Yes, ma'am." The driver pulled up to the curb in front of her brownstone.

She turned to Adam as the driver opened her door.

Adam was nodding and grinning like a damned fool. He put his hand over the receiver on his phone. "Anything else?"

The light filtered through the open door, glinting off his sunglasses. She tried to remind herself that this was the real Adam Langford—the flirt in the expensive car, doing whatever the hell he wanted to. He wasn't boyfriend material. He was a client, end of story.

"That's it. I'll talk to you tomorrow." She scurried out of the car before she could say something foolish, something like, "Please hang up the phone and forget that I ever came up with this stupid fake-girlfriend idea."

Melanie fumbled with her building keys. Why was the car still sitting there? It felt as if Adam's eyes were boring into her back. Finally, the lock turned, she stumbled through the door, and the limo pulled away. She longed for a measure of relief, but all she felt was confused and disappointed.

She trudged up the stairs to her second-floor walk-up. She'd moved in after Josh had dumped her. Even if she didn't miss him, she missed their old apartment. It was quaint and quiet, in the Chelsea neighborhood, with the best spot for reading on a Sunday afternoon, cuddled up on the couch. Luckily, that apartment had gone to a month-to-month rental, or she'd be stuck with that and her office space. The bad news was that they hadn't renewed the apartment lease because they were looking to buy a home, one big enough for a nursery.

Melanie rounded the railing to her door. Her neighbor Owen came down from the third floor, dressed for a run.

"You're back from your trip." He grinned wide and jogged in place, as if to remind her that he was in exceptional shape. Funny how his perfect physique did nothing for her except reassure her that she was out for more than a hot bod. She needed a companion. A partner.

She managed a smile. Owen was harmless, even if the way he kept tabs on her bordered stalker behavior. "Yep. Just now."

"Good to hear it. The building is too quiet without you around. Maybe we can see a movie this weekend."

He dipped his head to make eye contact, but she was nothing if not distracted by the thoughts of Adam whirring through her head—their near miss and the aftermath, the humiliating apology and her plan to keep herself on the straight and narrow.

"Um. Maybe," she answered. "We'll see. I'm in the middle of a huge job right now."

He nodded and smiled reassuringly. "Gotta keep the bills paid."

"You know it." *Understatement of the year, actually.* She unlocked the door to her unit. "I'll let you know if my plans change." With a quick wave, she bid Owen goodbye and let the door close. Exhausted, she leaned against it. Her apartment felt nothing like home today. It really just felt empty.

Seven

Every time Melanie opened the doors at Costello Public Relations, memories smacked her in the face. Time had dulled the pain, but it was still there—the betrayal of the man she'd once loved, the man who'd stuck her with the office lease from hell.

Things had once been perfect in this office, she and Josh working as a team, a devoted support staff around them. The sky was the limit, the future bright. She and Josh went home every night together, tired but satisfied. They were building something, and it felt wonderful.

They had made a vow to spend at least one hour each evening talking about things other than work. That typically made conversation difficult since their entire lives revolved around the business. The easiest thing was to fall into bed and make love. It wasn't fireworks, but it was an extension of their life together, inexorably wound together. They completed each other, or so she had thought.

She'd had no idea that the last eight months of their relationship were a lie. Josh was so good at faking it, so adept at putting up a facade that said everything was peachy keen, when in fact he was sneaking around, meeting another woman, romancing her, taking her to bed.

When she'd suspected that something was going on between Josh and their client, he'd dismissed it as preposterous. The flirtation, the rapport beyond the professional, was all in her head. The next thing she knew, he had a cold and was staying home for the day, when in fact he was emptying his things out of their apartment, hopping a plane to San Francisco and relocating with his new love, his "soul mate." Melanie didn't want it to hurt so bad anymore. It was exhausting.

She hurried past the unmanned reception desk. It'd been months since she'd been able to keep someone on fulltime. For now, it was better to run a tight ship, continue to build back the client list and come out on the other side stronger. That was the entire reason she'd done what she probably shouldn't have done and taken this crazy Adam Langford job in the first place.

She sat at her desk, quickly remembering that she hadn't made coffee. She sprang back out of her seat. Once that task was done and she had a steaming-hot cup of courage, she sat down to call Adam's dad, Roger.

"Ms. Costello," Roger's voice boomed over the other line. "To be honest, when I hired you, I was fairly certain that this would be the phone call where I would have to fire you."

Melanie swallowed. "Sir?"

"You know, the first check-in after you'd worked with Adam."

Right. Work. Adam. "The weekend went very well, Mr. Langford, I assure you."

"I hope I can count on you for complete honesty, Ms. Costello. I love my son very much and there's no one I trust more when it comes to business, but he has a verifiable lack of good judgment when it comes to the fairer sex. I trust that you kept to our agreement?"

How would she answer this? Find a technicality? She didn't have a choice. She needed this job and one could argue that she'd made only one mistake, even if it was a doozy—kissing Adam on the couch and losing all sense of time and space. "I stayed away from Adam's bedroom, if that's what you're asking." That much was the truth, but guilt still choked her. She'd not only violated the contract keeping her company in the black, she'd done the thing she told herself she'd never do—she'd become involved with a client. Thank goodness she'd had the presence of mind to stop herself. If Adam's lips had roved any farther, if she'd taken the chance to caress his bare chest, there would've been no looking back.

"Forgive me for even asking. It's just important to me that we keep things aboveboard." Roger cleared his throat. "I won't keep you, Ms. Costello. I spoke to Adam. He's very impressed with your work, which isn't quite what I expected to hear. He fought me hard on hiring a PR person, although he softened on the idea when your name came into the mix. As soon as he researched your background, he said yes. I suppose your reputation preceded you."

Melanie's mind raced. She knew Adam had fought the public relations campaign—he'd said as much himself. What he'd failed to mention was that he changed his mind after he found out she'd been hired. Researched her background… Her picture was front and center on her website and he'd said that he never forgot a woman, even though she hadn't anticipated that was his superpower. What went through his mind when he made the connection?

"Adam told me all about your plan with Julia," Roger continued. "It's a stroke of pure genius. Mrs. Langford and I adored her the first time we met her. Their romance was so short-lived, but maybe they'll see the error of their ways now that they'll be spending time together. Nothing like close quarters to kindle love's flames."

Kindle love's flames? Melanie's stomach churned. How would she make it through the coming weeks without wanting to take a nap on railroad tracks? "The press will eat it up, sir." *Will they ever.*

"Absolutely excellent, Ms. Costello. Looking at Adam's interview schedule, I'd like you to keep me apprised of the *Midnight Hour* appearance. I'd really like for that to happen."

She scribbled herself a note to make yet another call to the *Midnight Hour* producer, knowing the answer was likely still "we'll see." Adam was the right kind of guest for the late-night talk show—in the limelight, a "personality"—but their schedule was booked months in advance. "Yes, sir. I'm on it."

"Well, keep up the good work. I've spoken to my assistant. Your next check is on its way."

Melanie exhaled—money. That and a stellar endorsement from a man as powerful as Roger Langford was the reason she was doing this. Having to aid and abet Adam and Julia was merely the horrific trade-off. "Thank you, sir. I'll keep you posted."

It was only a little past nine thirty when she said goodbye, but she already felt as though she'd been at the office for days. Coffee. More coffee.

The next hour was spent catching up on other clients—a New Jersey real estate agent who wanted to build her profile with the well-heeled of New York society, and a hotshot chef in need of a PR campaign surrounding his nomination for a prestigious cooking award. After finishing her second cup of coffee, she got around to the mail—big, fat bills for her rented office furniture, internet, travel. Even the little things such as office supplies added up. When would every day stop feeling like one step forward, two steps back? She was a fighter and she wouldn't quit, but being a one-woman army was no fun.

The main office line rang. Melanie hated it when this happened, because it meant that she had to pretend to be the receptionist. She'd trained most people to call her cell phone, and many of her clients preferred email for communication, but her sisters still called the office when they needed her to deal with their difficult dad, and of course, new clients often placed a phone call first.

"Costello Public Relations," she answered. "How may I direct your call?"

"Melanie? Is that you?" Adam's warm, familiar voice did peculiar things, sending both excitement and nervousness pumping through her veins. "I hope your receptionist is out on a coffee run. The boss should never answer her own phone."

"I don't mind it every now and then." How she hated hemming her answers. "Did you lose my cell number?"

"I guess I just pressed the number for your office. Would you prefer I call your cell?"

"I want to make sure you can reach me."

"I take it you spoke to my dad?"

"Yes. About an hour ago." She wondered whether she should let him know that his dad had essentially asked whether or not they'd slept together. Surely it wouldn't make Adam feel better about their father-son relationship to know that the distrust when it came to that topic was so deeply ingrained.

"I told him about Julia."

"So I heard. He's very excited."

"Yeah, sorry about that. I suppose I should've warned you. He's thrilled by the prospect of me spending time with Julia. Don't worry, though. I gave credit where credit was due. It's all your brilliant idea."

I'm a veritable mastermind. "Thank you. I appreciate that."

"I wanted to let you know that I've worked everything out with Julia. We had coffee this morning."

"Instead of dinner tonight?" Apparently he just couldn't wait to start spending time with her.

"No. We're still having dinner. That's why I'm calling. I wanted to let you know where we'll be going and what time we'll be there."

"Oh. I see." She steeled herself. This was going to be her reality for the next several weeks, whether she liked it or not. Best to get used to it now.

"That's how this works, right?"

She shook her head to extricate herself from unpleasant thoughts. "Yes. That's right." She grabbed a pen. "Go ahead. I'm listening."

"We'll be at Milano. Reservations are for eight."

Only the most romantic restaurant in the city. "And Julia's publicist is okay with this?"

"Yes. Julia doesn't have another movie coming out for over a year. She'll do anything to stay in the papers, just so producers and directors don't forget about her. She's going to be thirty soon. That's ancient for an actress."

And yet she's still absolutely stunning. "Okay, then. I'll leak this to a few photographers."

"Great. Thanks, Melanie."

"And Adam, please don't…" Her voice cracked, breaking before the words she really wanted to say, which were "do this." "Please don't flip off any photographers."

"Don't you trust me to do the right thing?"

At this point, the person she didn't trust was herself. Her miracle fix for dazzling Roger Langford while making Adam less of a temptation was burning a hole through her stomach. Every time she thought about it, which was every moment since she'd told Adam her idea, it made her uneasy. Something about it was wrong, and she had an inkling as to what it was, but it was no fun to go there. If money and career were extraneous factors rather than center stage, she never would've asked Adam to spend more time with another woman. *Focus on the work.* "It's just a reminder."

Melanie hung up the phone and sat back in her chair, rubbing her now-throbbing forehead. If she was so brilliant, why did she feel like the biggest dummy on the planet?

Adam tapped away at his laptop, trying to fully express his ideas for a new app he wanted his development team to explore, but he was writing in circles. He dropped his elbows onto the desk and ran his hand through his hair. This entire workday had been a waste. He couldn't get his mind off Melanie.

How was he going to make the Julia thing appear real, and if he did, how would that impact his relationship with Melanie? His ego had been bruised in the mountains, but now that he'd had a chance to heal, he had to admire her tenacity, her devotion to doing her job well and aboveboard.

His assistant, Mia, leaned into the doorway of his office. "It's six thirty, Mr. Langford. You're supposed to be picking up Ms. Keys at seven and your car is waiting outside. With traffic, you'll be cutting it close."

"Thanks. Guess I'd better change." *And I need a drink before my first public outing with Julia.*

Adam closed the door to the private bathroom in his office and changed into a fresh shirt. He grabbed his matching suit coat from its hanger on the back of the door, and put on a black-and-gray-striped tie. *Here goes nothing.*

He wasn't nervous about seeing Julia. They'd had coffee and that had gone fine. The truth was that their breakup had been as amicable as could be. After three dates, Julia had grasped his hand in the back of the limo and said, "There's nothing here, is there?"

Adam had been immensely relieved. They liked each other. They could make each other laugh. But there was zero chemistry. On paper, they should have made the perfect couple. In reality, it all fell flat.

His real worry was whether or not they could pull off the charade of a romantic relationship. Surely people would see them together and know that they weren't *really* together.

He had to make it work, however much it contradicted the way he chose to live his life. It was in his own best interest to make the scandal fade away so his father could live his final days knowing for certain that the integrity of the Langford name was intact. It had to work to make Melanie happy, since so much of her job depended on it succeeding. In the end, if he was lucky, it would have one of two effects on her—it would either make her so jealous that she realized that she wanted him, too. Or it would help her see that he was a good man. This would be his audition, his opportunity to show Melanie what he was really made of. Hopefully that opportunity would help him ultimately make Melanie his.

The limo arrived at Julia's new apartment, and after a long twenty minutes of idle chitchat during the ride, they arrived at Milano. As Melanie had promised, a handful of photographers were out front of the restaurant.

"Julia," one of them shouted, "over here."

Cameras flashed as Julia held on to the tips of Adam's fingers. She knew how to work the situation, smiling enough to avoid an unflattering photo, but not enough to appear posed, walking just the right speed so they could get their shot.

One benefit of choosing Julia as his fake girlfriend was that she could take center stage. Even after the media inferno of Adam's scandal, she was still a bigger name. Her face had been plastered across national tabloids for years. Adam managed to hit the grocery store newsstands across the country a few times a year, not that he wanted the attention at all, but Julia was a fixture.

They strolled into the restaurant, dark wood paneling and white tablecloths as far as the eye could see. The gentle clinking of silverware and crystal stemware rose above a soundtrack of smooth jazz. The maître d' spotted them and whisked them to their corner table. Everyone in the restaurant gawked and whispered.

Julia consulted her menu. "So, sweetie." She glanced at him sideways. "What are you thinking about for dinner?" A bright smile crossed her lips and she knocked her head to the side, allowing her wavy brown hair to fall over her shoulders.

Any other man would've been drooling at her feet. Adam felt nothing. "Sweetie?" he whispered. "I don't think you called me that when we were dating."

She traced her finger on the tablecloth in a circle. "If we're playing a part, we have to do it right. We need pet names."

Adam nodded. "Oh. Okay." This would take some getting used to.

The waiter stopped by and took their drink orders—prosecco for Julia, bourbon, neat, for Adam.

He perused the menu again, not hungry for anything more than a good burger. "I guess I'll get the Tuscan rib eye."

Julia raised her eyebrows at him, imploring him to say what he'd forgotten to add.

"I guess I'll get the Tuscan rib eye, honey." He'd practically coughed out the word, a term of affection he'd never used for a woman. He wished he could've saved it for Melanie.

"Sounds great. I'll have the shrimp Caesar salad." Julia closed her menu and flattened her hand on the table. She stared at it, drummed her fingers then shot a look at Adam.

Oh. Right. He took her hand in his, but it felt wrong. This wasn't where he belonged. This wasn't the person he should be with. Of course, the person he wanted to be with, or at least have a chance with, had put him in this situation to start. So maybe it was best to just shut up, continue the charade and hope for the best. The LangTel gala was little more than three weeks away, and Melanie's assignment would be ending. He could try then. Try and possibly get shut down, again, but try he could.

"We should get our stories straight," Julia said once they'd ordered their entrees. "You know, how we got back together. People are going to ask questions. We need to have answers or it won't be believable."

Adam pinched the bridge of his nose. He was creative when it came to software and web applications, not when it came to making up stories. "Why don't you start?"

Julia sat up tall and smiled, an almost wistful look on her face. "I spent some time thinking about it today. I'm thinking that you called me when you heard that I was moving back to New York. Your life was in a shambles, of course. I mean, you'd really hit a low point."

Adam blinked, disbelieving what she said, even when it was the truth. "Uh, yeah. I get it." He shifted in his seat.

"We talked for hours on the phone that night and I agreed, hesitantly, to let you come by my apartment when I got into the city."

"Why hesitantly?"

"Adam, be serious. Of course I'd seen those horrible photos. They were all over the internet. What woman wouldn't be at least a little leery of you?"

His stomach soured. That could be one of Melanie's

doubts, too. She'd seen the worst side of him and been hired to show only the good. "I suppose you're right."

"You brought me flowers, white roses, I'm thinking, as a sign of good intentions."

"I thought white roses were for apologies."

"Well, you did break up with me."

"I thought we mutually decided to break up. And no one is going to believe that I broke up with you. That's absurd." He shook his head. Talk about absurd, this entire conversation was absurd.

"Okay, fine. Red roses. For passion." Julia winked at him flirtatiously.

Adam didn't say a thing. He just took a gulp of his bourbon.

"Sparks flew the minute we saw each other," Julia continued. "We knew that we had to get back together."

Adam leaned forward. "What do we say in a month when we end up breaking up?"

"Oh, the usual." Julia took a ladylike sip of her wine. "Two people devoted to their careers couldn't find a way to make enough time for each other. That's believable, right?"

A slow and steady sigh escaped Adam's lips. "More than you know, honey. More than you know."

Eight

The tabloid photos of Adam and Julia outside the restaurant on their first "fake" date were one thing—painful to look at, but tolerable. The shots of them having coffee a few days later were another thing—an odd ache cropped up in Melanie's chest, but she told herself it was heartburn.

There was hand-holding in the pictures. There were smiles. There were what might be construed as romantic glances. It was enough to make a girl give up all hope, which Melanie had already nearly done, all in the name of saving her business. But today, he was staring at Julia's butt. How much of this would she be able to take?

Fidgeting in her seat in the waiting room at Adam's office, she flipped open the newspaper, forcing herself to look at the photos of Julia and Adam running in Central Park with Jack. They looked so right together—smiling and running. It made her entire body hurt. After all, who smiles on a run? People ridiculously in love, that's who.

Adam and Julia were a perfect match on paper, as beautiful as could be. Adam, in particular, looked drop-dead gorgeous. Every woman in the city was probably gawking at these pictures. His gray Knicks T-shirt was stretched across his chest and stomach, taut enough that she could make out the subtle ripples of his abs. Oh, the kisses she'd bestowed on that magnificent stomach of his. The sensation of her lips on his skin still lingered. And now those abs were as off-limits as an entire cheesecake on a diet.

Hands down, the picture of the post-run stretch was the most painful. Julia, donning skin-tight black leggings and a similarly fitting tank top, was bending over, touching her toes. Adam, being a man, or at least Melanie was sure that would be his excuse, was ogling her butt. Julia had apparently received a free pass on gravity. *I could do five million squats and my behind would never look that good.*

Part of her wanted to take Adam to task over the photo since he was displaying the sort of behavior that had tripped him up in the first place, but the papers thought it was sexy, giving it the headline For His Eyes Only.

This was no way to start her day, not when she was about to spend the next two hours with Adam. Any minute now she'd be called into his office to help direct an online press conference, where he was set to speak with a dozen major business publications from around the globe via webcam. Today wasn't about the scandal. It was about putting the spotlight on Adam's business prowess, all to impress the LangTel board of directors.

She glanced at her watch. Adam was already five minutes behind on the schedule she'd given him. Luckily, she'd anticipated this and had given him the wrong time on purpose, just so that he wouldn't mess up.

"Ms. Costello, Mr. Langford will see you now," Adam's assistant, Mia, said, appearing from a door adjacent to the spacious lobby.

Melanie followed her through the door and down a wide

corridor as a steady stream of employees flowed back and forth from one open workspace to the next. The entire office was abuzz with people, countless staff, an army of Adam's choosing. She couldn't fathom the luxury of that much help.

Mia rapped on a door and opened it for Melanie. Adam's office was easily twice the size of Melanie's apartment—a luxurious yet modern space that was, like Adam, handsome and impressive. He was seated behind a sleek, black desk, phone to his ear, his back turned to her.

"We have the computer and monitors set up for the interviews." Mia pointed to a conference table on the far side of the room.

"Great. Thank you," Melanie whispered, not wanting to disturb Adam. She was taking a seat when he spoke.

"Hi there."

She glanced over at him. The instant their eyes connected, she was in trouble. It sent waves of attraction through her, which given the photos in the paper, only irritated her.

"Hi yourself." She wished she could've hidden the biting tone of her voice, but it was impossible. Her annoyance over him staring at Julia's miraculous butt wasn't going anywhere anytime soon. It would take a blowtorch to remove that image from her head. "This shouldn't last more than ninety minutes." She powered on the computer in front of her. "This has a webcam, right?"

"Of course. This is state of the art. What computer doesn't have a webcam?"

"Sorry. I didn't mean to insult your office equipment."

"You okay? You seem agitated." He grabbed that morning's newspaper off his desk and walked it over to her. "You've seen this, right? This is exactly what you wanted, isn't it? Everybody in the office was talking about it when I got to work. My dad called to tell me he loved it."

Melanie folded her arms across her chest. "Yes, I saw. Well done. Maybe next time don't get caught staring at her butt."

"Is that what this is about? Didn't like seeing that, huh?" Adam grinned like the damned Cheshire cat, taking a seat in the chair next to her. "Are you jealous?"

Melanie narrowed her focus, beyond perturbed by the question. "I'm trying to make you look like less of a womanizer, not more."

"Oh, come on." Adam shook his head, half laughing. "You can't be serious. Any man in the world would've done what I did. Her ass is spectacular. There's no harm in looking."

A heavy sigh left her lips, even when she didn't want him to see how much it bothered her. Did he have to use the word *spectacular*? It felt like a punch in the stomach. "Somehow I knew you would use the guy defense. I swear, men are so predictable sometimes. You see a pretty face and you just can't control yourself."

"Or a particularly attractive derriere, as the case may be." He leaned back in the office chair, arching both of his eyebrows at her, clearly enjoying himself. Mischief sparked in his steely eyes, even more compelling than usual when complemented by his deep blue dress shirt, tailored to flaunt every glorious inch of his chest and shoulders.

"Don't be cute. You have an interview to do in a minute. We can't be talking about this right now."

"Sure we can. They can wait. I want to know why this is bothering you."

"And I don't care to talk about it. You ended up in the newspaper with Julia. That's all I can ask."

The computer screen sprang to life, a grid of a dozen unfamiliar faces. The man in the upper right-hand corner waved. "Hello, Mr. Langford. Ms. Costello. I'll be moderating the chat today. We'll be ready to start in a few minutes."

"Sounds great. We're ready." Melanie neatly arranged her notes and pen.

"Actually, we're going to need about five minutes if that's okay," Adam said.

The moderator looked up from his desk. "Uh, sure, Mr. Langford. Just don't make it any longer than that. The journalists joining us today are all on a tight schedule."

"Don't worry. I won't hold you up." Adam reached over and muted the computer. "I want to know why the photo bothers you so much. Or do I have to remind you that it was your idea to fix me up with Julia?"

She hadn't been in close quarters with Adam like this in a week, and her mind and body were as conflicted as they could be. Everything about his physical presence—his smell, his hair, his hands—made her want to climb inside his shirt, while everything he was saying made her want to clasp her hand over his lips and tell him to shut the hell up. "Please stop reminding me that it was my idea. My brain can only take so much of this at one time."

"So much of what? Work? The photos? Julia?" He picked up a pen and flipped it back and forth in his fingers.

"Let's focus on the interview. You really don't want to know everything going through my head right now."

"Actually, I'd pay good money to know what's going on in that head of yours. We can start with the comment about men being so typical. Is there some jerky guy in your past? I mean, I'd like to think this is all about me, but now I'm wondering if there's something else going on."

She wasn't about to venture into the topic of her ex and her disastrous love life. "There's nothing more going on than me trying to do my job and you putting your special Adam touch on everything. It's like I spend hours setting a table for dinner and you walk by and turn the forks upside down. You thrive on making everything just slightly off-kilter, don't you?"

"Off-kilter?" He cocked an eyebrow. "How about real? I don't like things that are fake and contrived, that's all. I was spending time with Julia, she bent over, her butt is nice to look at, end of story. You don't have to read so much into it."

Then why can't I believe it's as simple as that? Melanie looked up to see the moderator waving at them both furiously. She turned the speakers and microphone back on.

"Mr. Langford. Ms. Costello. We really need to start."

"Yes, of course," Melanie said. "I'm so sorry for the delay."

Adam cleared his throat. "Yes, let's get started." He then began scrawling a note on a piece of paper. He slid it over to Melanie.

If you bent over in that skirt, I'd be happy to stare at your butt, too.

Nine

Adam let himself into his parents' Park Avenue apartment, the place he'd lived as a boy. It was opulently decorated, a bit stuffy for his tastes, but it was still home, crystal chandeliers, button-tufted sofas and all.

"Adam, darling." His mother swept into the foyer wearing her trademark look—black from head to toe with a vibrantly colored scarf around her neck. Adam couldn't remember a time when she'd worn anything much different, even when he was a boy.

"Mom. You look great." He kissed her on both cheeks, noticing that she'd lost more weight. The stress of caring for her ailing husband was taking its toll. "Is Anna here?"

"She's in the powder room. Should be out any second. We're having dinner in fifteen minutes. Margaret's making your favorite, beef Wellington."

"Sounds great. And Dad?" Adam and his mother strolled down the wide hall, shoes clacking on the black-and-white checkerboard marble floors.

"Watching television. He's developed a fondness for college basketball. Funny, since he never watched it before."

Adam had to smile, thinking about Melanie that night in the mountains. Even with the way it had ended, he would give anything to be back there with her right now—just the two of them, alone in that big house, the rest of the world a distant thought.

"Adam. My boy." Roger struggled to get out of his chair, but Adam knew better than to stop him, or worse, offer to help. The man was as stubborn as they came.

Adam hugged his father, who felt frail in his arms but still mustered a strong clap on Adam's back.

"Dad. It's good to see you." Every time he saw his dad, he had to wonder if this time would be the last. The thought was simply too sad to bear. He wanted to believe the doctors, and that Roger still had two or three months to go.

"And under such wonderful auspices, too. I couldn't be any more pleased with the way this public relations campaign has gone. Best money I've spent in years."

"Ms. Costello is very talented. No question about that."

Anna filed into the room. Her long dark hair was pulled back in a high ponytail. Always polished and professional, she wore a charcoal-gray suit and cream-colored blouse, having just come from her job as COO for a company that manufactured women's workout clothes.

Anna gave Adam an uneasy smile. Time with Dad was difficult for her. She was strong and independent, with a solid mind for business, but their father saw her in the context of their family—the only girl, the spitting image of her mother, a prized possession to be shielded from the harsh realities of board meetings and quarterly earnings reports. Roger Langford would never agree to let his little girl run LangTel, however desperate she was for the opportunity.

"Dad," Anna murmured, embracing their father. "You look good. Rosy cheeks and everything."

"That's because I'm happy. Adam and I were just talking about how well the public relations campaign is going. Your mother and I have two of our three children here for dinner. These days, I'm thankful for every little thing that goes my way."

"I actually heard from Aiden," Anna said, referring to their brother, the eldest of the Langford siblings. "He's somewhere in Thailand. I don't know much more than that. It was just a few lines in an email, and it'd been weeks since I'd reached out to him."

Their father shook his head in dismay. "God forbid that boy should call your mother and tell her he's alive."

Their mother's eyes grew sad. "He needs to stop avoiding your father's illness and come home."

"You know that's not going to happen," Adam said.

Aiden wasn't coming back anytime soon, not after the last argument he'd had with their father. No one dared speak of it, but Adam suspected it was about why Aiden was never considered to run LangTel and was left with little more than his personal shares in the company.

Aiden's upbringing was markedly different from Adam and Anna's. Six years older than Adam, Aiden had been sent off to boarding school when Adam was only two and Anna was a baby. Adam still didn't know why he and Anna attended private school in New York instead. He only knew that Aiden got into a lot of trouble at school—big trouble—and that Adam had been treated from a very young age as if he was the first-born. In many ways, it was as if Aiden didn't even exist, or at least not in their father's eyes. It saddened both Anna and Adam that they weren't close with their brother, but Aiden seemed content with keeping his distance.

"Anna, can I get you a drink?" Adam asked.

"Please. I've had a brutal day."

Adam stepped over to the bar in the corner to mix his sister a gin and tonic. She followed.

From the sound of things on the TV, someone had just hit a big shot in the basketball game. "Darn it all." Their father eased back into his seat. "I always miss the big plays."

Their mother consulted her watch. "Dinner should be ready in a few minutes. I'll check with Margaret and see how things are coming."

"You really heard from Aiden?" Adam asked Anna, careful to keep his voice low.

"It wasn't much. It's pretty clear he'd rather catch the plague than come home and face Dad."

"It'd be nice if they'd stop feuding." Adam shook his head, adding a jigger of Hendrick's gin to the glass and topping it off with tonic. "So what's the plan tonight? Are we going to talk to Dad?"

"Honestly, I don't know if I have the strength. If I have to listen to the speech about how I should be looking for a husband and thinking about private school for my unborn children, I might scream. Between Dad and my current job, I feel like I spend my entire life beating my head against a wall."

Adam drew in a deep breath. It was a miracle this subject hadn't given both his sister and him an ulcer. Ironic that they both had what the other wanted—he saw LangTel as a soul-sucking proposition, seeing out someone else's vision instead of his own. How he longed to have options like Anna.

She, on the other hand, would have done anything to become the first female CEO of a major telecom. More than anything, he sensed that she longed to prove herself, and do it on the largest stage imaginable.

Adam patted Anna's back. "I'll go to bat for you. We need to keep trying."

Margaret, the family's longtime cook, appeared in

the family room doorway. "Dinner is ready, Langford children." She smiled wide, looking like a pudgy Mary Poppins. For a moment, Adam could remember exactly what it was like to grow up in this household—every privilege a child could ever want, every expectation a young boy could never shoulder.

After dinner, Adam followed his father into his office, swirling bourbon in a cut-crystal old-fashioned glass. Since the cancer diagnosis, his dad had laid off the liquor. Roger took his place behind the massive mahogany desk, which had once been the prized possession of Adam's grandfather, the second Langford man to make a fortune in business. Even when Adam and his dad were having father-son time, the setup always more closely resembled a meeting.

"Tell me how things are going with Julia. I know you didn't want to talk about it in front of your mother, but you can tell your old man. You know, we actually look forward to seeing your picture in the paper now." He laughed quietly. "That's a big improvement from a month ago."

Adam wasn't convinced it had made things any better, at least not for him personally. Parading around Manhattan with his fake girlfriend made him feel like a human puppet, and for someone who had his own ideas of what he should be doing, that was uncomfortable. He settled into one of the leather club chairs opposite his father's desk. "Dad, I've told you. It isn't real. It was Ms. Costello's idea, remember?"

"I know what I saw in those pictures. You're happy together." Roger collected a handful of envelopes and neatly arranged them on his desk blotter. "Sometimes a man needs to open his eyes to what is already in front of him. You'd be a fool to pass up a woman like Julia."

All Adam could think was that the woman who was

already in front of him was Melanie. And she wanted nothing to do with him, at least not romantically.

"Julia is beautiful and famous, Adam. She's exactly the sort of woman your mother and I would love to see you with. You're a man. She's a woman. I don't see the problem."

The problem is that I don't feel anything when I'm with her. Adam took another sip of bourbon. His father was accustomed to getting what he wanted. Adam wasn't about to deny a dying man, but he wouldn't lie. "I need you and Mom to keep your feet firmly planted on the ground. Unless something drastic happens, there is no Adam and Julia."

"Son, let me ask you this. Do you know what I saw when I looked at you and your sister on the days you were born?"

Adam pursed his lips. "Wrinkly newborns?"

"I saw the future. I saw a boy to carry on my name and my legacy. I saw a girl to give your mother and me grandchildren."

"What about Aiden?"

"I thought I saw the future in him, too, but it turns out that I was wrong."

"Dad, don't say that."

"It's true. I have very few days left on this earth. The only thing I have left is hope that you and your sister and your mother will be okay after I'm gone. I need to know that you will have the lives you want. That means a husband for your sister and a wife for you. That means a roomful of grandchildren at Christmas for your mother." His dad's booming voice softened and wobbled. A single tear rolled down his cheek.

Adam sucked in a deep breath. He'd seen his father cry only once, the day his Grandmother Langford had died.

Adam knew that his dad had a heart as wide as an ocean, even if he could be stern and demanding.

"You can't worry about us like that. We'll be fine. And you have to stop assuming that you won't be around for those things, because you never know."

"I just need you to know that the three of you are the most important thing in the entire world to me. You're my only thought when I wake up in the morning."

Of course, Adam knew that his dad's statement wasn't entirely true. Willing to admit it or not, Roger Langford had an awful lot of ego wrapped up in the future of the corporation he'd built from the ground up.

"Dad, you know we need to talk about Anna and LangTel. You really hurt her feelings at dinner, and I don't understand why you refuse to see what an amazing job she'll do."

"It's not her abilities I question. I put her in charge of organizing the gala, didn't I?"

"That's not the assignment she was hoping for."

"She's a smart girl, but you have to be bulletproof to do my job, and I'm not willing to put my little girl in that position. It's my job to protect her. Call me an old man if you want to, that's just the way I feel."

Adam would've simply grumbled if he weren't so dead set on proving his dad wrong on this point. And it wasn't just selfish reasons that motivated him. There was more to it than his lack of enthusiasm for running LangTel. His sister had grown up in Adam's shadow, and he hated it. She was just as smart as him, maybe even smarter, innovative, quick on her feet. It was just that she'd had the unlucky lot of not being a boy. She was at an unfair disadvantage from the outset.

"Anna is as tough as any man. Maybe tougher. And you know, she helped me a lot when you put me in charge during your surgery and first wave of treatments. I don't understand why you won't give her the chance."

"You said it right there. She helped you. I can see her in a subordinate role. Perhaps she's senior assistant to the CEO or some such. You'll be at the helm, just as you've dreamed about since you were little."

Adam had to say what was on the tip of his tongue. "What if I don't want to run LangTel?"

The look on his dad's face was one of utter horror. "Don't let your sister's wishes cloud the issue. Of course you're going to run LangTel. That has been the plan from the day you were born, and I'm not about to stray from that now. End of discussion."

"Dad, I'm a grown man. I have my own company to run. You, more than anyone, must appreciate that I want to see my own vision come to life. I want to succeed with my own plans, not see out what you had hoped to do, but won't have the chance to." Dead silence rang through the room as Adam realized what he'd said. "Dad, no." He sat forward, placed his hands flat on his father's desk. "I'm sorry. That's not what I meant."

"You think I don't wish we were having this discussion because I was getting ready to retire? Because I do, dammit." He pounded his fist on the desk. "But I'll be gone by then. LangTel is my life's work and your mother's financial security, and you're the person I trust with it. So, like it or not, I need you to accept the fact that you were born to do this job. Period."

Adam sank back in his chair. How could he argue with his dad when he was facing death? He couldn't.

Ten

Most magazine editors were notorious for last-minute changes, and Fiona March, editor in chief of *Metropolitan Style*, was no exception. Adam's cover feature in the weekly magazine was one of the first things Melanie had put in place for the campaign, and it was easily her biggest coup. So when Fiona called her the night before and requested—no, begged—that Julia be present for Adam's interview and photo shoot, Melanie had no choice. Plus, Fiona had decided to conduct the interview herself, something she did only once or twice a year. Melanie had to make it happen.

Great. Can't wait to hang out with Mr. and Ms. Beautiful.

Melanie blew out a breath, staring at the numbers above the elevator door. She considered pushing the alarm. The temptation was so great that her hand twitched. A screeching siren would at least delay her arrival at Adam's penthouse apartment and create a diversion. If she was super lucky, maybe they'd send a hunky fireman to her rescue and she could have a fling with him and forget Adam. Firemen made good boyfriends. They didn't complicate a woman's life, and especially not her career.

Much to her dismay, she hadn't had the nerve to press the red button, and the doors slid open when she reached Adam's apartment. This was her first time here since their night together, and visions were already flashing through her mind. To make matters worse, her stroll down memory lane would be accompanied by her first meeting with Adam's new "love interest," Julia. *Breathe. Breathe.*

The last time she'd been in this room, she was half-undressed, Adam's hands all over her while she frantically unbuttoned his shirt, nearly breaking the zipper on his pants, before embarrassingly stepping on his foot. He'd played it off so sexily, too, sweeping her into his arms and mumbling into her ear, "No more walking for you." A minute later, her hair was splayed across his bed and he was blazing a trail of kisses down her stomach. Just thinking about it created waves of pleasant warmth, followed by emptiness. She'd needed him so badly that night. She'd needed him in the mountain house. What was it about him that elicited that response?

A *Metropolitan Style* photographer was busy capturing the open-plan living room—high ceilings, dark wood floors, cool gray walls, brown leather furniture just as Adam liked it. There were the more feminine touches now—a cashmere throw, decorative candles and objets d'art on the coffee table, all added by the home stager Melanie had hired and to which Adam had protested. The neon beer signs and moose head were indeed fiction.

As much as she wasn't thrilled to meet Julia, she needed to be here to make sure this interview went perfectly. She needed to be here to give Adam the stink-eye if he started down the wrong path with his answers. She scanned the room, catching sight of Adam perched on a tall wooden stool in the corner, Jack at his side.

She hurried over, admiring him in the icy blue shirt she'd convinced him to wear. It wasn't lavender, but at least he was taking direction. He was ridiculously handsome in the lighter color, even when the look on his face was one of distinct misery. "It's okay to smile, you know," she said.

The male makeup artist working on Adam cast Melanie a knowing grin. "I'll be done with him in a minute. I don't think he's enjoying it."

"I just want to get this over with," Adam mumbled as he had concealer applied to the corner of his mouth. "I've had about a dozen important emails in the last five minutes. This is seriously the last thing I have time for right now."

"I made him put down his phone," the makeup artist said. "It was making him wrinkle his forehead, which makes my job pointless."

A vaguely recognizable female voice rang out behind Melanie. "I think he looks perfect. Handsome as ever."

Melanie turned, coming face-to-face with the most stunningly gorgeous nightmare she'd ever seen.

"You must be Melanie. I'm Julia." She held out her hand, flashing the smile that had graced dozens of movie posters. Her shoulder-length brown hair glinted with auburn highlights, her minimalist makeup flawless. And then there was her outfit.

Julia burst out laughing. Her stunning green eyes grew wide with surprise. "Oh my goodness. We're wearing almost exactly the same dress. Neiman Marcus? Last fall?"

If Melanie could've done anything at that moment, she would've gladly taken her chances with the elevator alarm. "Ha. Oh. Wow. Yeah. Funny." *Kill me now. Please.* "Mine is vintage. It belonged to my mother."

"Oh, how wonderful. Even better that you have a story to go along with it." Julia tucked her hair behind her ear.

Julia's voice had a sweet edge that instantly put a person at ease, except Melanie refused to be at ease. She was too busy feeling Adam's eyes on them, knowing he had to be studying how she measured up to the picture-perfect gazelle wearing nearly the same outfit.

"Turn around, so I can get a look at you." Julia looped a circle in the air with her finger.

Melanie's stomach sank when she caught the smirk on Adam's face. This bore far too much resemblance to the things her father used to make her do—twirl around in a fancy dress for the neighbors, look pretty for company. Melanie's sisters were always far better at it than she was, just as Julia was when it came to showing off the sublime lines of her black wool dress.

"I promise you, you aren't missing anything." Melanie internally begged for all attention to be taken away from her. Especially when she was forced to stand next to a woman with four percent body fat and not a single pinch-able inch.

"I'll tell you one thing, you fill out the skirt so much better than I do." Julia perched on the back of Adam's leather sofa.

Melanie would've gasped if she weren't so dumbstruck. *Fill it out?* Any woman would've wondered if Julia was using girl code for *fat*. Melanie knew for certain that she wasn't fat, but she was no waif either. She had curves—real hips, a real butt.

"She does look fantastic in it, doesn't she, Jules?" Adam chimed in.

"Perfection. Makes me think I need to take mine to a tailor." Julia crossed her mile-long legs.

Now Melanie was beyond confused. Julia hadn't meant it as an insult? Maybe it was easy to be generous with compliments when she was always the most beautiful woman in the room, wherever she went.

The elevator into Adam's apartment opened and Fiona March, willowy with short black hair, made her entrance. She was juggling a large designer purse and an oversize bottle of water. "Melanie, so glad you're here already. Sorry I'm late."

Melanie rushed over. Fiona was one of Melanie's most important contacts. "You're never late. You're right on time."

"You're sweet," Fiona answered. "You're also a terrible liar, but so was my third husband and he was fantastic in the sack, so I'll give you the benefit of the doubt."

Melanie laughed, leading Fiona across the room. "Let me introduce you to Adam and Julia."

The three exchanged niceties, but Adam seemed distant, as if something was bothering him. She pulled him aside while the cameraman adjusted the lighting for the photos they would take during the interview.

"Are you okay?" Melanie looked up at him, trying like hell not to get caught up in his eyes.

He cracked half a smile, which was better than most men's full smile. "You're so sweet when you want to be."

I always want to be sweet. My job doesn't always afford me that luxury. "I just want to make sure you're okay. You're my client. I need you to be okay."

"Ah, so that's what you're concerned with. Whether or not your client is going to perform for you today."

"Not exactly. I'm genuinely worried." She pointed at his forehead. "The makeup guy was right. You get this little crinkle between your eyes when you're thinking too much."

Adam rubbed the spot with his fingers, as if to erase it. "I do? No one has ever told me that before."

"Probably from staring at a computer screen all day long. You need to give your eyes a break every now and then." She reached out and grasped his elbow. "Let me know if you need a minute, okay? It's better to take the time to collect yourself now, rather than later. I don't want you to be caught in an uncomfortable situation."

Adam cast his eyes to his arm, where Melanie was holding it so tenderly with her elegant hands. He'd almost forgotten the way her touch brought him to life. Her sweet smell washed over him, her curves in that black dress called to him, reminding him where his hands fit best, the places she loved to be squeezed.

She patted him on the shoulder. "Everything okay?"

He nodded. "Yep."

"You'll do great. Don't worry."

He fought a smile. Even though it didn't seem to go beyond their professional relationship, she cared. Sometimes she cared too much about things, about what other people thought, in particular, but she was passionate, and that was so damn sexy.

It tormented him to see her in this room, in his apartment, knowing the things they'd shared the first time she was here. Those few hours were engraved in his memory. She'd made him laugh, she'd made him growl with desire, she'd made him feel something strong and real, when that had been missing from his life. He'd never had that kind of instant chemistry with anyone, not even with his ex-fiancée, and he'd been deeply in love with her. Logic said that he could have that with Melanie, but it took two to tango, and she'd shown she had no interest in dancing.

He could still remember Melanie's words from their night together, as she wrapped her legs tightly around his waist, her slick heat inviting him inside for the first time. She'd arched her back, rolled her entire body into his, grasped the back of his neck with both hands and murmured in the sexiest voice he'd ever heard, "You feel like a dream." If he closed his eyes, he could still hear her say it, and that made everything in his body grow tight and hot.

Sure, women had lauded Adam with praise, but much of it was meaningless—things about having an amazing apartment or looking hot in his suit or having an air of power and control, whatever that meant. Melanie had chosen a simple line, sweet and almost poetic, that was all about him as a man, the things he could give to her that had nothing to do with money or prestige. His God-given talents.

"Adam," Melanie said.

"Yes?" She was still close enough to pull into his arms and dammit if his hands didn't want to do exactly that.

"Fiona is ready to start the interview."

Adam forced a smile. Showtime. All he could think as he took his place opposite Fiona was that as soon as he was asked about his relationship with Julia, this would all become real, at least to the world. The photos in the tabloids were largely conjecture. This would make it seem authentic, and that made him wish he could stand up and tell everyone but Melanie to leave.

"So, Adam." Fiona leaned forward and placed her hand on his knee. "May I call you Adam?"

"Of course."

She smiled warmly. "Tell me about your rekindled romance with Julia Keys. We've all been seeing you two around town together, and I'm sure our readers would love to know more about the hottest couple in Manhattan."

Okay, then. Right into it. Adam cleared his throat, on edge, torn between what Melanie would want him to say and what he wanted to say in front of Melanie if he had the chance. "What can I say? Julia is a lovely woman and we're having a great time becoming reacquainted." If only he could spout the reality, because what he really wanted to say was, "Well, you see, the truth is that I went from casually dating dozens of women to having a fake girl-friend while pining for a woman who wants me to remain her client."

"Can you tell us about how you got back together?" Fiona asked.

Adam shifted in his seat, tugging at his collar, remembering the script Julia had given him at the restaurant. "Well, I heard that Julia was moving back to New York and I wanted to see her, so I called her." Out of the corner of his eye, he could see Melanie hanging on every word. Was he doing what she wanted? He thought so, but he'd been wrong before. "She agreed to let me come by her new apartment when she arrived in the city. That was the start of it."

"Don't forget about the roses," Julia blurted, stepping forward and placing her hand on Fiona's shoulder. "I'm sorry to interrupt, but I must. You see, Adam is so romantic, and he doesn't give himself credit."

"Tell me more," Fiona said. "Actually, Adam, if it's okay with you, I would love it if Julia joined us for the interview."

Adam shot a look at Melanie, who had her arms folded squarely across her chest. He had no earthly idea what she was thinking. "Perhaps we should ask Ms. Costello."

Melanie nodded. "Sure. Of course. Whatever seems right, Fiona." Her voice wobbled when she spoke. Perhaps this was as nerve-racking for her as it was for Adam.

"Can we get a chair for Ms. Keys, please?" Fiona asked.

Julia perched herself on Adam's chair and draped her arm across his shoulders. "Don't worry about me. I'm just fine like this." She wiggled herself into place against him, making him exponentially more uncomfortable. "So, yes, Adam brought me a dozen roses that night. At first it made me mad, because roses seemed like such a cliché."

Adam wanted to scream. *The damn roses were your*

idea. Instead, he forced himself to watch Julia as if he was captivated by her every word.

Julia shrugged and pressed a kiss to Adam's forehead. "But it was so romantic, I couldn't do anything but tell him that yes, I wanted to get back together with him, too. It's been like a dream ever since."

Except that it wasn't a dream, at all. It was a big, messy lie that he was expected to perpetrate.

Plus, Melanie had called him a dream, and that was the only context in which he ever wanted to think about that word again.

Eleven

Melanie's email and voice mail had become the Julia and Adam show, and she, its unwitting choreographer.

Everyone had questions. *Is it true that they're serious?* How was Melanie supposed to answer that? It appeared so. The photos were heartbreakingly convincing. Even when Melanie was supposed to *know*, deep down, that they weren't really a couple, it looked as if they were. Why else would she get a pit in her stomach every time she saw them in the newspapers together?

Is he finally settling down? His family sure seemed to think so. Roger Langford had called and thanked Melanie again for her supersmart plan. The Langfords had reportedly hosted Julia for dinner and she regaled everyone with her wit and Hollywood stories. Adam's mom had apparently remarked that Julia and Adam would make beautiful babies. Of course they would…not that Melanie could stand to think about that for even a minute.

Will Julia be the woman to tame him? Melanie audibly

snorted when she read that one. Tame Adam Langford. It made him sound like a lion in the circus, when she knew that he was nothing of the sort. Not even when he'd been engaged had Adam allowed himself to be anything less than the person who called the shots.

Her cell phone rang and she was about to chuck it across the room, especially when she saw on the caller ID that it was Adam. Spending the past three hours dwelling on the question of whether or not the relationship between Adam and Julia was real had left her in no mood to converse with the man in question. But she had to answer.

"Adam, hi."

"I'm coming to your office." The sound of car horns blared in the background.

"What? Where are you? When?" Melanie closed her eyes and pinched the bridge of her nose. "Why?"

"Aren't you full of questions? I'm in the car, stuck in traffic, and late for the interview with that tech magazine. We're about a block from your office. I just had my assistant call the writer and tell him to meet me there. It actually works out better for him, anyway."

Melanie surveyed her disastrous desk. The lobby area was fairly tidy, but there was one glaring thing missing—someone manning the actual reception desk. How does someone run a so-called up-and-coming public relations firm with no staff? She had absolutely no idea, only that she had to do it every day.

She scrambled to put on a pot of coffee and arrange a suitable interview space in her reception area for Adam and the writer. The final throw pillow on the sofa had been fluffed when Adam strolled in.

"Sorry. Crazy day," Adam said, hitting a button on his phone and shoving it into his front pocket. He was dressed in impeccable gray flat-front trousers and a black dress shirt with the sleeves rolled up to the elbows, no tie. The dark stubble along his jaw was at its usual perfection. It was a windy day in the city and Adam's hair showed the effects, disheveled and mussed, just so—sexy and enticing, almost like bed head.

She had to clasp her hands together, squeeze them hard, all while gritting her teeth to keep from combing her fingers into the thickest part of his hair, at the top of his head, where it got a little curly when it was wet. It was no wonder he had such a pull on her. Why did he have to be so flawless? Well, he did have one or two flaws, the most glaring of which was his unwillingness to make a serious relationship with a woman a priority.

Adam scanned the reception area. "Where is everyone?"

"Everyone?" She turned, forcing herself to keep from drifting closer to him after catching a whiff of his heady scent.

"Your staff. Receptionist. Assistants. Interns. I had visions of a busy office like mine. Your client list is a mile long."

It used to be a lot longer. When Josh was here. There had been a lot of things when Josh was still there— someone to share the workload, someone to talk to about her problems, someone to hold her at the end of a long day and tell her that everything was going to be all right. Her support system, her safety net, was gone.

If she'd had the strength to put the right spin on the merits of a one-woman operation, she would have, but she'd spent her morning creating spin. Putting a glossy shine on everything she said to Adam was exhausting. It was so much easier to be honest. "It's just me right now. Lean and mean. Makes things a lot simpler."

"Oh. Okay." He seemed skeptical despite the affirmation, furrowing his brow. "But who runs the office? Who buys office supplies and fixes computer problems? And what about things like arranging your travel or organizing your calendar or hell, even the little stuff, like making appointments to get your hair cut or running to the dry cleaners?"

When he had to put it like *that*, it made it all sound impossible, so utterly absurd. "Maybe my life isn't as complicated as yours. I work all day, I go home and sleep. Rinse. Repeat."

"Sounds boring."

It is.

"And a little unfulfilling," he had the nerve to continue.

"It isn't, thank you very much. It also makes it remarkably easy to keep myself out of the tabloids."

Awkward silence hung in the air. "Ouch."

She felt horrible. "I'm sorry. That was out of line."

"Just seems like you'd get a lot more clients, and bigger ones at that, if you had a staff to take care of the little things. You need to delegate if you're going to be successful." He was not about to let this go.

"Follow me. I need to get you guys some coffee. Unless you'd prefer water."

"Definitely coffee. I need the afternoon pick-me-up."

Melanie stalked into the state-of-the-art office kitchenette, twenty times nicer than what she had in her apartment and just as expensive, to finish cobbling together some hospitality, yet another of the many hats she wore. She removed a lacquered tray from the cabinet, spread out a white linen napkin and topped it with a sugar bowl and pitcher of cream. Two teaspoons were added to finish it. "Will you want anything to nibble on? I have a few different kinds of cookies in the pantry. Or I could run down to the bakery and see what they have for pastries."

"See? Like this. You should not be doing this. You're a smart, capable businesswoman and you work hard. You should not be worrying about cookies and pastries for a client."

Did he really see her that way?

He leaned against the black granite counter, his hand close to her hip—so close he could've touched her with little effort if he'd wanted to. "I'm not wrong."

Oh, he was all kinds of wrong, only in that he was a little *too* right. Ideas swirled in her head, of a hot kiss in the break room, his insistent lips on hers. Maybe he'd back her up against the refrigerator with enough force to flatten the back of her hair, maybe even hard enough to make the magnets fall off the door. If that ever happened, he wouldn't hesitate to untuck her blouse and snake his hands along her back. He'd unhook her bra, mold her breasts in his hands. She'd have no choice at that point—she'd have to take off every stitch of his clothes so they could send each other into blissful oblivion. Or she could slam on the brakes, as she had in the mountains, because a tryst with Adam in the kitchen, or anywhere else, would be wrong.

Melanie's eyes fluttered. Her face flushed, her chest burned. She'd have to stick her head in the freezer if she allowed herself any more daydreamy latitude. No more Adam fantasies. Not today.

She filled two mugs emblazoned with Costello Public Relations. What a joke. Her company was hardly custom coffee cup–worthy in its current state. Adam had insinuated as much. "Anything else, Mr. Wizard? Should I be taking notes?"

"Very funny. Mr. Wizard. I'm just giving you a little free advice. I do know what I'm doing, you know." He claimed one of the coffees from the counter and added a splash of cream. "I made my first million out of a dorm room. I know how to grow a company."

"You know how to grow *your* company. We're in two completely different lines of work. Believe me, I know how to grow mine." Sure, she could snag a lot more clients if she didn't have to worry about things like vacuuming the office before meetings. It didn't matter. She simply didn't have the means. She'd have to work more and sleep less until that turned around.

"Okay." Adam headed out of the kitchen and back into the reception area. "We can talk about it later. I'll take you out for a drink after the interview. One of my favorite neighborhood bars is around the corner."

"A drink?" *Just what I need. Liquor to fog up my already questionable resolve.*

"Yes. I know it falls outside the scope of going to work and going home, but I think you'll enjoy yourself. We haven't spent enough time together that wasn't related to work."

"We'll still be talking about work. I think that counts."

"Something tells me we'll get around to other topics."

Other topics. Melanie did not want to discuss her family or her love life. What else was there? The weather? She made a mental note to check the forecast online while Adam did the interview. Maybe she'd brush up on NBA scores, knowing that Adam followed the Knicks. Anything she could launch at him to steer the conversation toward the benign. If he brought up Julia, she wanted to be prepared to change the subject, pronto.

There was a knock at the door and a lanky man opened it. "I think I'm in the right place. I'm looking for Adam Langford."

"Yes, you're in the right place," Melanie answered, smiling and rushing across the room to shake his hand. "Please. Come on in. I made coffee."

Twelve

This was as close Adam could come to taking Melanie out on a date, at least while he was in a fake relationship with another woman. And at least while Melanie was dishing up roadblocks and mixed signals.

He opened the creaky, dark wood door of Flaherty's Pub for her. "Ladies first."

She grimaced, peering into the dimly lit bar. "Something tells me they aren't going to want to make me a mojito in this place."

"Sorry, Buttermilk. Nothing with a sugared rim, either."

She pointed at him accusatorially, pursing her lips, but he caught a fraction of a smile. "You know how I feel about that nickname."

He ushered her ahead. "I do, but the problem is it fits you so perfectly. A little sweet, a little sour. Most of the time I can't think of anything better to call you."

"Adam Langford, you're lucky I need a drink so badly."

His favorite watering hole in Manhattan was dark as

could be—poor lighting, worn mahogany, deep maroon upholstery on the booths. A jukebox predating them both sat at the back. A few regulars were lined up at the bar. They'd probably spent their afternoon knocking back a cold one, preserving the lost art of conversation.

Melanie clutched her purse to her chest. "This isn't what I imagined when you said you'd take me out for a drink."

Adam shook his head, placing his hands on her shoulders. "Relax. Don't you trust me? I've been sneaking in here since I was a teenager. I love it. It's totally different from anywhere else I spend my time. My parents would be appalled if they knew about it."

Jones, the gray-haired bartender, flipped a towel over his shoulder and nodded at Adam. "Look who's here. The prodigal son returns." Jones had long called him that, but he knew little about Adam's background. He never asked, Adam never offered. Coming to Flaherty's was time for throwing darts and leaving everything else behind.

Adam laughed and curved his hand at Melanie's waist. "Come on," he said quietly. As much as she looked out of her element, she did trust his taste enough to follow his lead across the room. Adam shook Jones's hand. "How are you, my man? Business treating you right?"

Jones pushed his black-framed glasses up onto his nose. "I've got every microbrewery in the country trying to get me to sell their beer, but for the most part, I can't complain." He wiped a spot on the bar with a towel. "Where are your manners? Are you going to introduce me to the lovely lady you brought to my fine establishment?"

Adam nodded. One thing he loved about Flaherty's was that nobody gave him a hard time about anything serious. There was no speculation about him or his character. They certainly wouldn't know what was playing out in the tabloids. Jones, especially, was concerned with the sports page and not much else. Here he could be single Adam Langford

and he could take Melanie out for a drink. "Yes, of course. This is Melanie Costello. Her office is about a block from here. I'm surprised you two haven't run into each other."

Melanie smiled, seeming to warm to her surroundings. "Probably just on different schedules."

"Jonesy, I need you to make Melanie a very special drink. She loves mojitos. Anything you can get close to that?"

Jones scoffed. "Are you kidding me? I spent two years in Puerto Rico after I was in the military. I make the best mojito ever. My wife grows the mint out at our place in Staten Island."

Melanie saddled up to the bar, perching in a swivel stool and crossing her splendid legs. "That sounds wonderful. Tell me about your wife. How long have you been married?"

"Her name is Sandy. Been married twenty-seven years. Not counting tomorrow, of course." Jones winked at Melanie as he got out a pint glass.

What the hell? "How did I not know you could make a mojito?" Adam asked.

"Maybe because you never ordered one." Jones went to work, muddling mint and sugar in the bottom of a cocktail shaker. "Maybe because you never ordered anything more than a bourbon or a beer. And maybe because lovely Melanie is the first woman you've ever brought in here."

Melanie rested her elbow on the bar and turned back to look at Adam. She flashed her beguiling blue eyes. "The first woman ever. I feel so special."

He knew she was being sarcastic, but he loved bringing out that side of her—the sassy, flirtatious side. It made his entire body tight, especially everything below the belt. He opted not to sit next to her, instead draping his arm across the back of the bar stool. Here, in a place where he could be anonymous, he didn't mind allowing his mind to wan-

der to thoughts of what it would be like to be with Melanie. To have her as his girlfriend, or more.

In that world, he could deal with his other problems in a much better fashion. If he had Melanie, she would understand his work stresses. She would understand at least some of his family stresses because she'd dealt with similar things herself. And damn if she wouldn't be a sight for sore eyes after a long day.

Jones finished up their drinks. "I'll put yours on your tab, Adam. Melanie's is on the house." He again winked at her, which elicited an uncharacteristic giggle.

Adam wasn't shocked by Jones's attempt at flirtation. How could a man not be drawn to Melanie? Aside from her beauty—deep blue eyes and soft pink lips, curves designed to make him lose all sense of direction, and that was only the start—she had something within her that was simply magnetic. There was her staunch independence and her fiery devotion to her work, but she also possessed vulnerability. There was a caring and gentle woman inside, as well.

Melanie stirred her glass, poking at the ice with her straw. "Jones, this is delicious. Absolutely the best I've ever had, and I've had more than my fair share of mojitos."

Adam drank in the vision as Melanie skimmed the corner of her mouth with her tongue and flashed a satisfied grin. He had both feet firmly planted on the ground and still he felt as if he might fall over. "Let's take one of the booths in the corner," he said.

"Keeping her all to yourself?" Jones asked.

"I'm no dummy," Adam replied, taking his drink from the bar.

They settled into the small, half-round booth, Melanie placing her large purse squarely between them.

Damn. He'd been counting on a chance to inch closer. "Talk to me about Costello Public Relations. I want to

know how you can run a one-woman shop. And don't tell me you're keeping it lean and mean. I don't buy it."

Melanie cocked her head to the side. "What is so mystifying about the concept? I'm capable. I get stuff done."

"I never said you didn't. I only said that you'd get more done if you had support staff. You must be bringing in enough money. I know how much my dad is paying you and it's substantial."

The sound that came out of Melanie was equal parts frustration and resignation. "Let's just say I'm upside down in my office lease and I'm still paying off the furniture." She shook her head and took another long draw of her mojito. "If you must know, that's the real reason I don't have a staff. I can't afford it. Yet." She planted her finger on the table. "Someday I will."

"Why'd you spend so much money on your office? You had to have had a business plan, a budget for the first few years."

"It was my former business partner's idea."

"So sue her."

She paused before she answered, seeming to calculate what to say. "Sue *him*. And it's not that simple."

"Sure it is. You have to be ruthless when it comes to things like this. It's just business."

"It's not just business." Melanie took a sip of her drink that was so long, he thought she might make it all the way to the bottom. "It's personal. Very personal."

Whatever was very personal was also clearly a sore spot. Maybe she didn't like talking about work after hours. It wasn't his intention to draw her into an unwelcome conversation, especially now that they finally had the chance to go out together, but he had to know.

"I'm listening. Tell me everything."

"I'd rather not talk about it."

He fought disappointment that she still didn't trust him

enough to simply come out with it, but he had to keep trying. "Please don't be afraid to confide in me. I'm only trying to help. No judgments. Just help."

She looked him in the eye, searching, for what he did not know. He took the opportunity to reciprocate, scanning her lovely features, his heart heavy that she was obviously suffering over whatever had happened.

Finally, she sighed and dropped her shoulders. "My business partner was also my boyfriend. I thought he was about to become my fiancé, but I was clueless. He had an affair with one of our clients, while he and I were living together and talking about marriage and children." Her voice wobbled, but her resolve was still evident. "He left with her. For San Francisco. They went into real estate together. And unfortunately, I trusted him and it's only my name on the lease, or anything for that matter. Costello PR is all mine. Sink or swim."

Anger bubbled under Adam's skin. He hadn't been in many fistfights in his life, but he wouldn't hesitate to flatten Melanie's ex, to make him feel a fragment of the pain he'd caused her. "I'm so sorry. Talk about a double whammy."

He was about to reach across the table and take her hand, but she pulled it back, picking up her drink and downing the last of it.

"A triple even," she muttered when she came up for air.

"An affair. With a client…" And there it was. Aside from the contract with his father and her extreme attachment to doing things her way, there was another reason to keep him at arm's length.

"Yes, Adam. An affair. With a client. It looks a little different from the outside, doesn't it? Some people would call it unseemly."

Adam wanted to protest, to say that it wasn't the same because this excuse for a man, her ex, was a coward. And he had to be certifiable. Why would anyone leave her? "The way he went about it, it does. It wouldn't have to be like that. If two people were attracted to each other, they could wait until the working relationship had come to a close and then proceed with romantic intentions."

"But both people would have to be unattached, completely, for real." Something wouldn't allow her to say that she meant Julia. "And both people would have to be capable of commitment. Because I don't do casual. It's not in my DNA."

Did this mean she was interested? And could he do commitment? Could he start out a relationship that way? Usually he eased into that mode, knowing he'd likely never get there, but Melanie deserved far more. "Are you giving me a checklist?"

"Even if I did, it still wouldn't account for *my* checklist, and trust me, mine is a mile long."

Adam's phone beeped with a text. *Dammit.* Just when he was learning the landscape of the epic battle to win over Melanie. "I'm sorry. I should've put it on vibrate."

"It's okay. I understand."

Adam cringed as he read the message from Julia.

I need you at a dinner Saturday. Director in town.

It turned out that the fake relationship benefited Julia more than they'd originally thought it might. She'd landed a gritty role as a mouthy Long Island mob wife, a part her agent said she wouldn't have been considered for before she got serious with a man immersed in controversy. Julia was convinced this was her chance at industry awards.

The text was an unwelcome reminder of what was waiting for him outside Flaherty's—obligations that revolved around other people's needs, all of it keeping him from Melanie, and just when he'd convinced her to open up. She knew so much about him, even the bad things. He didn't know much beyond Little Miss Buttermilk and now, her bastard of an ex.

"Crisis in the office?" she asked.

Adam clicked off his phone and shoved it into his pocket. "Just something that will have to wait." He smiled, relishing his return to conversation with Melanie. "Where were we?"

"Nowhere. I'd like a change of subject." She looked over her shoulder. "Or a turn with the jukebox." She whipped back and dug through her purse. "Shoot. I don't have any change."

"The machine takes quarters. I'll get some from Jones."

"And another drink?" She lifted her glass and shook it at him.

He laughed quietly. He adored her playful side, especially since she didn't show it often.

Melanie slid out from the booth and wound her way to the jukebox. Adam got change and another round of drinks, listening dutifully as Jones informed him that he was a "certifiable idiot" if he did anything less than treat Melanie like a princess and figure out a way to make her his wife. For the moment, he was going for a successful first date.

Adam watched the sway of Melanie's hips as she stood before the jukebox, pushing the button and making the records go by. He would've done anything for the chance to walk up behind her, wrap his arms around her waist and kiss her neck. But even in the place where they could shut out the world, he wasn't sure she'd be amenable.

"About time," she said when he reached her. She plucked the quarters from his hand and plugged the machine, then tapped away at the numbers.

"Don't I get to pick any?" He moved in next to her until they were standing virtually hip to hip. He had several inches of height advantage, even when she was wearing heels. Heels that he couldn't help but notice made her legs look incredible.

She grumbled. "I don't even know if you have good taste in music." She turned to block his access to the number pad controlling the jukebox.

You clever minx. "You've got to be kidding. I have excellent taste in music, and don't forget that I financed this endeavor. I at least deserve a turn."

She punched in another number. "Okay. You can pick one song. But it'd better be good." With a flourish, she stepped back, placing the tips of her graceful fingers on her collarbone.

Give me strength. Adam's head was doing somersaults. When Melanie let down her guard, when she was being sassy and independent and sexy, exactly the way she'd been the night he first met her, he had no logical thought other than getting her into his bed, ASAP. He chose a song with little deliberation, so little that he didn't remember what he'd picked.

"What's your song? I didn't see."

"Um. It's a surprise."

Melanie swirled her drink with the straw. "I could drink about seven of these, but then you'd have to put me in a cab because I would either be asleep or very, very stupid."

"I don't want you to drink that much, but I'm willing to go along with whatever you want tonight."

Melanie cast him a smirk. "You ready to put your money where your mouth is? Because I want to dance."

Adam knew exactly where he wanted to put his mouth, squarely on hers. "This isn't really the place for dancing." Flaherty's customers were accustomed to their feet sticking to the floor. It wasn't exactly the place to bust out a box step.

"Maybe we need to change that." She grabbed his hand and placed it on her hip.

She was lucky his fingers didn't have a mind of their own because her dress had a tie at the hip, and that was precisely where she'd placed his hand. That stretch of cobalt blue knit would be gone in two seconds flat if his hands were in charge.

He took her other hand, wrapped his fingers around hers, bringing her right next to him with a decisive tug. "What if I told you I don't dance?" He led her in a small circle on their impromptu dance floor, sliding his hand to the small of her back. His hand fit perfectly.

"I'd say you're a liar," she muttered, following him in their back-and-forth sway. It was only the slightest of surrenders, but he'd take what he could get. Every last drop.

"The truth is that I really don't like to dance, but I like this. A lot. At least I can have you in my arms."

"Is three minutes long enough? That's how long a song is, right?"

"We put in two dollars. I bought myself a good twenty-four minutes if my math is correct."

"If you play your cards right, I'll stick around that long."

Adam laughed quietly. "You and I are exceptionally good at talking in circles around each other. Neither one of us wants to give in and say what we're really thinking."

Melanie looked up into his eyes, unafraid. "So just tell me, Adam. Tell me what you're thinking." Maybe her bravery was born of the mojitos, but he'd have to match it with his own bravado.

He sucked in a deep breath, steeling himself, hoping this wasn't going to make her put up an even bigger wall between them. The last time he'd been honest about his feelings, she'd done exactly that. "I'm thinking that you're beautiful and smart and sexy and fun to be with. I'm thinking that any man who would walk out on you is a moron. I'm thinking that I might not be much better for spending time with Julia when I could be trying to build something with you."

Her lashes fluttered as she seemed to wrestle with what he'd said. "Wow."

"Too much?"

"Um, no." She shook her head. "I'm just surprised."

"By what part? Surely you know how I feel about you. Surely you know that I'd take a chance with you if I had one."

"And to what end? So we can date for a week or two and you can get bored of me?"

His heart pounded fiercely. If he'd ever been bored with a woman, it was only because she wasn't the complete package. She wasn't like Melanie. "I would never get bored of you. Ever."

"How am I supposed to believe that, Adam? Even when you were engaged, she didn't manage to hold your interest."

Thirteen

Roger Langford was paying Melanie a significant sum of money, but her job description didn't include party-planning duties. She took on the extra work partly because the annual LangTel gala also raised money for charity. The other half of the equation was that all of her work with Adam led up to this one night. It had to be perfect. She would do everything she could to make sure that it was nothing less.

Several minutes late and fighting a monster headache, Melanie rushed into the grand ballroom where the gala was to be held. Anna, Adam's sister, was already there.

Anna smiled and shook Melanie's hand. "Thank you for meeting me and helping out. I'm a fish out of water with this sort of thing." Her long chestnut brown hair, the color exactly like Adam's, was pulled back in a high ponytail. Also like Adam, she was confident, but hers was more reserved than cocky. Her demeanor exuded grace and professionalism.

Melanie placed her bag on a table, wishing she'd taken more pain reliever before she'd left the office. "It's not a problem. I have a fair amount of experience organizing parties. Every now and then I end up doing one for a client."

Just thinking about the gala made the corners of Melanie's mouth draw down. That night would spell the end of working with Adam. He'd go back to his life, she'd go back to hers. As to what that entailed, she wasn't sure. She'd thought once or twice that maybe she and Adam could go out to dinner once her assignment was over, although she wasn't sure how that would work either. Did she have the guts to ask him out on a date? Sitting around and waiting for him to do it would be torture. Not that it would matter. For all she knew, Julia and Adam would be running away together after the party.

The two women walked the opulent space, going through the notes Roger Langford's assistant had given them. Table linens, decor and menu had been decided months ago. It was really Melanie and Anna's job just to discuss how the flow and timing of the party would work, since Roger would be making his big announcement and Adam making the closing comments.

"An hour for cocktails should be sufficient, I think," Melanie said. "I'll make sure the media has an unobtrusive spot to view everything. Your dad gives his speech, which I hope will be short." Her phone rang, but she let it go to voice mail.

Anna let out a breathy laugh that said she didn't find it funny. "Don't bet on that one. My father loves the sound of his own voice."

"I already need to work with Adam on what he's going to say, so I'll coach your dad, as well. If he goes too long, the networks will chop it up for broadcast. There are already enough misperceptions about your family. We don't need to add to them." In her planner, Melanie scribbled down a reminder about the speeches. "After that, Adam takes the stage and addresses everyone, we have a toast and dinner is served."

"The king will have ascended to the throne."

Precisely—Adam's long-awaited chance to take over his father's massive corporation. "It is almost like a coronation, isn't it?"

Anna nodded slowly. "From everything my mother says, my father has been waiting since the moment Adam was born for this to happen." Her voice faltered, but she wasn't choking back tears. As near as Melanie could tell, Anna had extreme command of her emotions. "Of course, we all thought it would happen when my dad retired. We never imagined it would be because he's dying."

Melanie's heart ached for Anna, and for Adam, as well. Watching their father fade away had to be so difficult. Did it make things easier that Roger had opted to keep the severity of his illness a secret, or had that added to the family's burden? Adam didn't always talk about it, but she'd seen how much it weighed on him. "I can only imagine how hard this must be for you." Her phone rang, but she let it go to voice mail again. If only there was more she could say, or something she could do to make it better, but it was an unsolvable problem. They'd be lucky if Roger Langford lived to see another Christmas with his family.

"Thank you," Anna said. "I'm not really sure why my father put me in charge of the final party details, aside from the fact that he felt like he needed to throw me a bone. And I'm a girl. There's that, too."

"Throw you a bone?"

Anna looked up at the ceiling. "I'm surprised Adam hasn't told you, considering how much time you two spend together. I've been lobbying to take Adam's place since before my dad got sick. I'd like to be the one to carry out his vision for LangTel. Unfortunately, my dad's logic is straight out of the 1950s. He only approves of me in business if I'm shopping for a husband while I do it."

Melanie had no idea that the sibling rivalry between Adam and Anna was so intense that they would be at odds over running the company. As much as she wanted Adam to take his rightful position, she sympathized with Anna. "My dad treats me the same way. He's just waiting for me to fail, so that he can tell me that he told me so. Of course, that only makes me want to work harder to prove him wrong."

Anna smirked. "Exactly. Do you have any idea how hard I worked at Harvard to beat Adam's GPA? Just so I could show my dad that I was equally capable?"

"I can only imagine. Your brother is a smart guy. I'm sure his grades were nearly impossible to beat."

"Tough, yes. Impossible, no. I did it, but it wasn't by much."

Melanie's phone rang for the third time. "Somebody really wants to get a hold of me. I'm so sorry."

She held up her finger while Anna mouthed, "No problem."

"Hello? This is Melanie."

"Ms. Costello, this is Beth, one of the producers for the *Midnight Hour*. We've had a last-minute cancellation on tonight's show. One of our guests has fallen ill. Is Adam Langford still available? We'd love to have him if he is."

Melanie glanced at her watch. "What time?"

"Can he be here in an hour for hair and makeup?"

Oh, crap. "Yes. Of course. We'll be there."

Two hours after Adam received the frantic phone call from Melanie, he was ready to walk out in front of the *Midnight Hour* cameras. Almost ready. "I don't know what's wrong with me. I can't stop sweating."

Melanie waved a magazine in front of his face. "You're going to have to find a way to stop. By sheer willpower or something." Judging by the expression on her face, she was as horrified by his physical state as he was.

"Maybe if I'd had more notice." He wished he hadn't sounded so annoyed, but he was still bothered by the things she'd said when they'd gone to Flaherty's a few nights before.

Yes, he'd made mistakes when he was engaged. He knew better now, even if no one seemed to believe him. And Melanie's suggestion that he'd get bored with her was absurd. Part of the reason he was so drawn to her was because he was certain she'd never bore him. Still, he had to admit that she had reason to bring it up. There'd been a time when women went through a revolving door in his life. Her comments weren't completely unfounded.

"Relax," she said, working hard to convey calm. "It's going to be fine."

"You don't understand. I never get nervous. It's an omen or something." Adam ran his hand through his hair.

"Stop messing with your hair. You'll make it look weird."

He groaned under his breath. "Do you realize that I'm about to go on a show that millions of people watch? People who expect guests to be funny and charming and clever." Why had he agreed to do this? This was not what he did. He was always in control. He was always in charge. He didn't allow himself to fall prey to circumstances, but being on this show—the lights, the audience, the host—made him feel as if he was about to do exactly that. "I can't perform on command."

Melanie smirked. "I don't enjoy seeing you uncomfortable, but I do like seeing a chink in the armor every now and then." She firmly placed her hands on his shoulders. "First off, you need to take about ten deep breaths. Second off, you need another shirt. I'm not letting you go on television in the one you're wearing." She strode over to the garment rack in his tiny dressing room and picked out what was supposed to be a backup. "Take off your shirt."

"This is no time for sex."

"Okay, Mr. I Can't Be Funny and Charming on Command. You're going to be fine. Now take off your shirt so we can get you out there."

Adam unbuttoned, distracting himself with the vision of Melanie. Every inch of his body warmed to the idea of doing this with her, taking off clothes, for real. In his fantasy, she did the unbuttoning. Always. How disappointed his body would be when he had to break the news. Melanie didn't take him seriously when it came to romance. Her career and her company were her first priority, and it would be hypocritical to blame her—he'd suffered a broken engagement for the same reason.

Melanie grabbed deodorant from the dressing table and thrust it at him. "This reminds me that we need to decide what you're wearing to the gala. We need something that will look perfect in pictures and on television. We can do it when we go over your speech."

"Uh, okay. Sure."

"Mr. Langford?" The stage manager leaned into the room, clipboard in hand. "Five minutes until you're on." She then seemed to realize the problem. "You have thirty seconds to get that shirt on or I'm going to go into cardiac arrest. Makeup is on their way for touch-ups."

Melanie shook out the shirt and held it for him. "I'll button the front. You do the cuffs."

The makeup woman whizzed into the room. She tucked two tissues into his shirt collar and dabbed at his face with a large cosmetic sponge. "You're sweating," she remarked, pursing her lips. "You need to stop doing that."

"He'll be fine." Melanie cocked her head to the side,

finishing the buttons. "He's so damn handsome, the camera will love him no matter how sweaty he is."

He knew she was just trying to distract him, but his heart felt lighter to hear her say something like that. He couldn't help it.

The makeup woman whisked away the tissues around his collar. "That's as good as it's going to get."

Melanie straightened his shirt, brushing his shoulder. "You say you're nervous, but you're really not. I've had clients who were far more on edge than you. You make it look like a piece of cake."

"If I'm not nervous, it's because of you."

The look she gave him—sweet and kind, edged with skepticism—was enough to make him forget all time and place. "You're going to be great. I know you. You'll knock 'em dead."

When was the last time someone had said something like that to him? "You're amazing. I don't think anyone else would be this patient with me."

"I have complete confidence in you. I never doubt your ability to do anything."

He leaned forward, grasped her elbows and kissed her on the temple. "Thank you."

"You're welcome." She nearly leaned into the kiss, placing the tips of her fingers on his chest. She peered up into his face then shied away with a blush that would've made a rose envious.

The stage manager poked her head into the dressing room. "Mr. Langford. You're on." She led them down the short hall to the stage entrance.

He took a deep breath. If he didn't stop thinking about Melanie, he'd have more than a sex scandal to explain on national TV. He conjured one of his most unpleasant memories in hopes of stemming the tide of blood flow between his legs. "I haven't been this nervous since I ran for class president in sixth grade."

"Oh, please. I'm guessing you were formidable even at eleven years old."

"Are you kidding? It was a disaster." He looked back over his shoulder before he stepped between the gap in the velvet stage drapes. "I lost by a landslide."

Melanie had prepared herself for the worst. What a waste of time.

The instant Adam was out under the studio lights, he turned on his irresistible charm and the entire world fell under his spell, or at least everyone watching in that studio. Melanie knew very well what it was like to get swept up in Adam. The audience never stood a chance.

The host, Billy Danville, didn't hesitate to poke fun, starting the interview by donning a tiara that spelled out "Princess" in glittery rhinestones above his head. "So, Adam. I understand there's been a scandal."

Three weeks ago, Adam wouldn't have been able to take the joke. He would've rolled his eyes in disgust and admonished everyone in that room for caring about the personal life of someone they didn't know.

Not today. Adam didn't flinch. He sat back in his chair, a wry smile on his face. "Has there been a scandal? I've been so wrapped up in college basketball that I hadn't noticed."

The audience laughed. The host laughed. Melanie chuckled a bit as well, but mostly she was in awe of Adam.

"But, seriously," Billy said, thankfully ditching the tiara, "it looks like you've put the scandal behind you. We've all had a chance over the last few weeks to get to know you from the various interviews you've done, which is great. We know now that you're not just a ridiculously handsome tech whiz, but that you also have a fondness for staring at your girlfriend's rear end."

"The great American pastime," Adam countered.

Billy smiled. "Indeed. You know, *just* this morning, I was thinking I should spend more time looking at your girlfriend's rear end."

The crowd erupted again.

"But seriously, tell us about your relationship with Julia Keys," Billy continued. "Things are looking pretty hot and heavy in the newspapers. Are there wedding bells in the future?"

Wedding bells? Melanie held her breath, unsure how Adam would answer, unsure what she *wanted* him to say. With every passing day, his relationship with Julia continued to look real. And that was what she'd wanted, wasn't it? She'd asked him to make it convincing. She'd practically shoved him into Julia's arms.

Adam shifted in his seat. "No. No wedding bells, despite what the tabloids want to speculate about."

"Everything's good, though?"

"Oh, sure. Everything's great. What can I say? Julia is a beautiful, smart and talented woman. Any guy would be lucky to spend time with her." On that topic in particular, Adam seemed as calm as could be.

Billy nodded eagerly. "Of course. I mean, give her my number in case she gives you the heave-ho."

Adam continued to roll with the punches, taking the jokes at his expense, handling every sensitive subject, and there were many, including the things his ex-fiancée had said about his ability to commit, and ultimately, the question of his father's health.

Billy gathered a stack of index cards in his hands. "I hate to bring this up, but there are an awful lot of rumors that your father's illness is much worse than we've been led to believe."

Adam pressed his lips into a thin line. "You know, my dad is receiving excellent medical care. He's in great hands. He's as sharp as a tack, stubborn as a mule, and still goes into the office every day."

All true. All glossing over the reality, the one the Langfords wanted to hide. Adam had learned to handle the tough questions flawlessly.

"And at what point will you be taking over LangTel?" Billy asked, not seeming to notice that Adam hadn't really answered his question.

"If that ever happens, it's still a ways off. I try not to focus on it too much."

"What was it like growing up in the shadow of such a formidable man?"

"You know, if I stand in the shadow of my dad, I'll never measure up. That's something I've come to realize over the years. He wants me to be just like him and we are alike in many ways, but I have to be my own man, as well. I can see where he's coming from, though. If I had a son, I'd probably want the same thing."

By the time Adam was offstage, it felt as though a massive weight had been lifted. His appearance on the *Midnight Hour* had been a triumph. She couldn't have been any more proud.

"Well? I did okay, huh?" he asked. The smile on his face said that he knew very well he'd done far better than okay.

"Spectacular. I couldn't have scripted you any better if I'd wanted to."

"This calls for a celebration."

"Flaherty's? We can't really go anywhere else without you being seen." She strolled down the hall with him to his dressing room.

"We need champagne and Flaherty's is not the spot for that." Adam flashed her a look. "I was thinking my apartment. Just a nightcap. It'll be fun."

Adam's apartment. Champagne. Melanie could see danger signs in her head. He was a temptation when she was mad at him—she couldn't imagine mustering a shred of resolve when she was ready to nominate him for Man of the Year. "It's late. You have work tomorrow, I have work."

"And as far as I'm concerned, we've been working all night. We deserve a break and a celebration. I promise I'll be a perfect gentleman."

"Why do I have a feeling you think you're always a perfect gentleman?"

"I don't need to think it. I am."

Fourteen

Pop. Champagne bubbles fizzed and sparkled as Adam filled two glasses. Maybe it was the high of having aced his appearance on the *Midnight Hour*, but it felt as though every sense was heightened. Or perhaps it was having Melanie in his apartment, alone.

Melanie clinked her glass with his. She sipped her champagne, vivid blue eyes gleaming. The look on her face was so familiar and damning—flirtation, invitation. It only made him want to try, again, even when it could end with her hand squarely in the center of his chest, her supple lips muttering, "I can't."

"You really were spectacular tonight. Truly," she said.

He unbuttoned his shirt cuffs and rolled up the sleeves, feeling as on top of the world as he'd felt in a long time. He'd kicked ass tonight, but more important, he and Melanie had kicked ass together. "Thank you, but it was all your doing. If you hadn't gotten me centered before I went on, I could've easily flopped." He trailed Melanie as she wandered into the living room.

"I knew you were going to be great." She waved off his comment. "I always had complete confidence in you. We might disagree from time to time, but I always know one thing. When you say you're going to do something, you do it."

Whenever life or work got messy, a lot of people's confidence in him seemed to waver—his father, the board of directors, even his own company had been tough on him lately. When it came right down to it, when push came to shove, Melanie had unequivocal faith in him. It was like a universal truth to her, a closely held belief.

She leaned against the frame of one of the tall windows, the city lights bringing out her singular radiance.

"And what if I said that I was going to kiss you?" he asked, acutely aware of his breathing. "Would you believe that, too?"

"Adam. You know that's not what I meant."

"But I want to. That's all I can think about. That's all I've thought about since we went to Flaherty's. And now, looking at you in the moonlight, seeing you in that dress, remembering exactly how well my hand fits in the curve of your back…"

"That sounds like a lot more than a kiss."

"If we do it right, then yes."

She kept her eyes set on the city. "What about Julia?"

"She isn't what I want."

She laughed in a sweet, hushed tone. "I'm going to need more champagne to believe that. You said it yourself tonight. Any man would be a fool not to want to be with her."

He shook his head. "No. I said that any man would be lucky to spend time with her. It's not the same thing."

"You've learned the art of the spin all too well."

He grasped her shoulder, urging her to look at him.

"Please tell me that you know it isn't real. This was your idea. It was all your plan."

She turned and studied his face, as if searching for the answer, when he was already giving her everything exactly as it was. "You said it yourself. You aren't good at pretending. I've seen you two together. It looks real."

"Pictures are only as real as the newspapers want them to be. You should know that better than anyone."

She knocked her head to the side, releasing a wisp of her delicate scent. "I guess."

"Pictures in a newspaper don't make a relationship. You need a connection."

"I know that. I do." She nodded, but her eyes still showed doubt. "It's just that it's so convincing."

He shook his head again. How would he get her to believe? "It's all Julia's doing. I'm only following her cues. She's not the one I want. You are."

Melanie reached out and took his hand. It was as if the earth stopped moving. "Maybe it's the words that are tripping me up. Maybe I need you to show me."

He took the champagne glass from her other hand and set it on the table, never taking his eyes off her. "I've been waiting to show you. All I want to do is show you." He cupped the sides of her face with both hands, cradling it and gazing deeply into her eyes as his fingers caressed the silky skin of her neck. The blood was coursing through his body like a raging river. If there was any justice in the world, he would have her. It was the most basic and undeniable need he'd ever endured. "Let me show you all night long."

Melanie's breath caught when Adam lowered his head and kissed her. His mouth on hers was arresting. There was no mistaking what he wanted. He claimed her, and it electrified her, right down to her toes. She needed him closer and she pressed into him, craving his heat, arching into him, molding her lips to his as their tongues circled.

Weeks of holding back had her about to jump out of her own skin. She wanted to savor every touch, and at the same time nothing was happening fast enough. She frantically unbuttoned his shirt. "Watching you change tonight was torture." She dragged her fingers across the flat plane of his abs, spreading her hands upward to his chest, eagerly crossing the small patch of hair and across to his firm shoulders, pushing the shirt to the floor. Even just having her hands on his skin was heaven. "All I wanted to do was touch you."

"Just being around you is torture. I can't think straight half of the time."

He took her into his arms, holding her tight, the warmth pouring into her from his bare skin. It felt so right. He had her exactly where she was meant to be. It ushered in a war of relief and hunger deep inside her belly. Push and pull. Give and take. Her mind couldn't help but obsess over finally having what she wanted, what she'd spent the past year wishing she hadn't walked out on—Adam.

He kissed her neck with an open mouth, unzipping the back of her dress and tugging it forward, his knuckles grazing her shoulders. It was one of the most expensive items of clothing she owned, and she couldn't have cared less. She let it drop to the floor like a wet towel after a shower, then started on his belt.

He stopped her with his hands. "Not here."

Her chest wobbled, as if someone had plucked a single string of a guitar. Was it his turn to be sensible and sane? Because for once, she wanted them both to be weak at the same time, both of them to give in. No more *shouldn't*. No more *can't*. "Please don't tell me you're turning me down," she said breathlessly, her hands still on his belt buckle.

"Never. I just want you in my bed. I've waited long enough to make love to you. I want it to be perfect."

He took her hand and led her through the living room, down the corridor to his bedroom. "Much better," he muttered, gripping her waist with both hands and easing her back onto the bed. "I need to look at you." Pale moonlight filtered through the windows, casting a glow around him. His eyes raked over her body. "You're so beautiful, I'm having a hard time wrapping my head around it."

She couldn't tear her sights from him either—his chiseled jaw and broad, defined chest called to her in every way. She wanted her hands all over him, his all over her, and then she wanted him inside her.

"Enough looking, Langford. I need you now." Scooting to the edge of the bed, she sat up and rid him of his belt and pants. Every inch of him was rock-hard, especially what was right before her. She eased his boxer briefs past his hips, pressing the heel of her hand to the base and wrapping her fingers around his length.

Adam closed his eyes and groaned, clutching her shoulders then pushing her back onto the bed. He lay down beside her, rolling her to her side and unhooking her bra. He took the puckered skin of her breast into his mouth, sucking her nipple gently as he shimmied her panties down her hips. Goose bumps spread across her skin like a wildfire through the underbrush, anticipation now at a full boil. There was nothing else in the way. Their legs tangled, they bucked their hips against each other. Kisses came hot and fast and everywhere.

"Let me get a condom," Adam said breathlessly, reaching for the bedside table.

"I'll put it on." She wanted every chance she had to touch him.

He handed her the foil pouch. "Have I mentioned that you're perfect?"

"No, you haven't." She pushed him to his back, straddling his thighs, relishing the delight on his face as she took care of him. "So say it again."

Adam chuckled quietly. "I thought we decided that I should show you." He pulled her shoulders down to him and kissed her like he was making up for lost time and lost opportunities, passionately and deeply. "I need to feel as close to you as possible."

Melanie lifted her hips and reached between her legs, taking him in her hand, guiding him inside. In that instant, it seemed as if neither of them took a breath, him filling her while she sank down and her body molded around him. By the time they succumbed to oxygen, they were one, and there was no having enough of each other.

Kisses came at full tilt as they rocked back and forth in a perfect rhythm. Pleasure coiled tightly inside her. The way he swiveled his hips built the pressure at a rate that her body struggled to keep up with. She knew the release would have her holding on with both hands. She'd waited so long for this and it was finally happening. Adam set every fiber of her being on fire—just like the first time, except so much better, because she knew him on a deeper level now. They had history.

Adam rolled Melanie to her side, threading his fingers through her hair, kissing her softly as he took long, slow thrusts. She hitched one leg over his hip, bringing him closer by pressing against his back with her calf.

"You feel so incredible," he said between kisses. He swept his lips across her jaw, down her neck, stopping at her breast, which he gathered in his hand and squeezed, making the already tense skin harden. He licked and sucked, sending her barreling toward her peak.

His breaths became uneven. Hers were ragged. She was so close. The dam was about to break. Adam doubled his efforts, driving harder until she knocked her head back and gave in to rolling waves of bliss. Light flashed in her mind—a supernova, magnified.

Adam quickly followed, calling out as his body froze before he shuddered with his own release. He pulled her snugly into his arms as their breathing slowed. He kissed her forehead gently, again and again.

Was this real? Was it all a dream? She gave in to the warmth of Adam's body and the tender caress of his unforgettable kisses. For the first time in a long time, everything was not only right—it was real.

"That was incredible," Adam said. "Everything I've waited for."

"Spectacular," she replied, kissing him and running her fingers through his very messy hair.

"I have to say one thing, just so we're clear."

Melanie's heart jumped. What was he going to say? "Yes?"

"You're not going anywhere. I don't want you to leave after what we just shared. I need you to stay the night."

Contentment took hold again—he wanted her to stay. But just as quickly she realized the ramifications. "Are you sure that's a good idea? There could be photographers outside your building. That'd be bad if I'm seen leaving in the morning."

"Then we scope it out. I'm not letting you out of my sights. Tonight, you stay here. With me. The whole night. Deal?"

What was the old saying about going for broke? She'd already done the thing she'd sworn she would never do and it had been so worth it. If something went wrong, she and Adam would deal with it, together. For now, they had each other, and they had the whole night. "Of course I'll stay. The whole night."

Fifteen

Melanie awoke feeling as if she was floating inside a daydream. Did last night really happen? The morning sun beamed through Adam's bedroom windows. She clutched the sheets to her chest. Adam's sheets. Adam's bed.

The distinctive sound of paws on the hardwood floor filtered into the room and Jack appeared. As soon as he spotted her, he rounded to her side of the bed.

"Good morning, buddy." She rolled to her side, facing Jack.

He lowered his head, begging for scratches behind the ear, which she was all too happy to provide.

"Don't you two make an amazing pair," Adam said from behind her.

Melanie looked over her shoulder, drawn to the sleepy warmth of his voice. He knocked the breath right out of her, wearing gray pajama pants loose around his hips, no shirt, holding two coffee cups.

"Good morning." It was impossible to fight her grin—he was too damn sexy.

He set his knee on the bed and leaned down to kiss her forehead. "Morning, beautiful." He handed her a mug. "Cream and one sugar, right?"

She nodded, incredulous. "You remembered." Of the millions of things Adam had crammed in that gorgeous head of his, how he'd managed to remember the way she took her coffee was beyond her.

She blew gently on the coffee and took a small sip, feeling, well, conflicted. Last night had been absolutely glorious, and it had felt so good to finally surrender to him, but there was no question it had been born of a moment of weakness. She'd been so caught up in the moment, so swept away by Adam and weeks of telling herself she couldn't have him.

And she still didn't have him, even if she was fairly certain now that the illusion of Adam and Julia was exactly that, an illusion. He wouldn't have slept with her if Julia was a genuine love interest. The Adam she knew would never do that. The Adam of urban legend might, but that wasn't the real him.

What was first and foremost on her list of concerns was the contract with his father. She'd made a pact with herself to honor the agreement, and she'd broken it. She hated making excuses. She hated the notion of giving herself a free pass or letting anything slide, and yet that was the only way around what she'd done.

"I wish we could spend the morning in bed." Adam placed his coffee cup on the bedside table and crawled under the covers with her. "But I have a ton of meetings, starting at nine. If it was only one or two, I'd move them."

"Meetings." Melanie's heart thundered in her chest. "Oh my God. What time is it?"

"A little after seven. Don't tell me you're late for something this early."

"I have a nine-o'clock, too. But I have to get all the way down to my apartment, shower, change, then get to the office and make coffee. I'll never make it if I don't leave right now." She threw back the covers, quickly realizing she had nothing to cover herself with. She grabbed a pillow and shielded her body, scanning the floor for her bra and panties.

"It's a little late for modesty, Buttermilk. There isn't a square inch of you I didn't reacquaint myself with last night."

"Can you please help me find my underwear?"

He reached to the floor on his side of the bed, producing the garments. "I don't get to keep these as a souvenir?"

She scrambled over and snatched them from his hand. "Very funny." She pinned the pillow to her chest with her chin and tugged on her underwear. She wasn't exactly sure why she didn't want Adam to see her naked right now. Perhaps it was the unforgiving nature of sunlight. Or worse, the unforgiving nature of guilt. "I have to get my dress."

She cast aside the pillow and hurried out to the living room. Adam followed her. Seeing her dress and shoes cast aside on the floor brought back a flood of memories, the way she had felt when he'd rubbed her cheek with his thumb and placed that impossibly soft kiss on her lips, the heat of his hand on the bare skin of her back, the way he filled her so sublimely. It was all so perfect and all so wrong.

"Hold on two seconds," he blurted as she wrestled on her dress. He shook his head, smirking as if she were crazy. "For God's sake, let me do the zipper."

She turned, but that sense of Adam approaching her

from behind, knowing that her stretch of back was exposed to him, sent a zillion goose bumps racing over the surface of her skin.

Zip. He quickly grasped her shoulders and pulled her close, her back to his chest. "Talk to me." He delivered the words straight to her ear in a low, tone that reverberated in her body. "I can tell that you're panicked, and I need to know why. I have a feeling it's about more than a meeting."

Hearing his voice, her body wanted nothing more than to be naked with him all day, especially when his warm breath brushed the tender spot behind her ear. Her brain, however, was waging a counteroffensive, about to force her to blurt something about needing to leave, which meant her poor heart struggled for itself, stuck in the middle. "I just…" She sucked in a deep breath. How many times had she uttered these words? Surely Adam was tired of them. She sure as hell was.

"You just what? You're just worried? That what we did last night was wrong?"

She blew out a deep exhalation. "Yes." There was nothing left to say. He'd boiled it down to its essence.

He turned her around and pulled her into a hug. "I understand." He rubbed her back reassuringly. "Listen, we both know that this isn't ideal, but we have nothing to be ashamed about. I wanted you, you wanted me. It's as simple as that."

"But your dad. The contract."

He only reined her in tighter with his arms. "Don't worry about my dad. He'll never know a thing." He kissed her forehead. "Now, let me walk you downstairs and put you in a cab so you aren't late for your meeting. I'd have had the doorman arrange for a car if I'd known you needed to be out the door so soon."

Melanie reared back her head, shaking it. He was being

so sweet. And so stupid. "What if someone is outside your building? Photographers?"

"I'll call downstairs and make sure the coast is clear. The doormen are extremely efficient at clearing away the riffraff by now."

"You call, but I'll go by myself. It's safer that way." Her stomach wobbled. Sneaking around was so far outside her comfort zone.

"What kind of gentleman would I be if I didn't escort you downstairs?" He scrubbed the scruff along his jaw with his hand. "Tell you what. I'll ride with you down to the lobby. I won't take no for an answer."

Melanie collected her things while Adam made the call. He threw on a sweatshirt and slid his feet into a pair of running shoes, leaving the laces untied. They stepped onto the elevator, no words between them, but Adam took her hand, rubbing it tenderly with his thumb.

Melanie's head swam. What were they doing? Was this a one-time thing? These were questions that needed to be asked, but there was no time for answers, at least not this morning. And regardless of the answers, he had to continue with the charade of Julia at least through the gala. How would she handle that emotionally if she and Adam were even entertaining the notion of romance?

Nothing about this insane situation bode well for a genuine, long-lasting relationship anyway. She could see it now, their children asking how she and their father had met. *Well, Daddy had a fake girlfriend because Mommy told him it would get him good publicity, and your grandfather didn't want us to even touch each other, so of course Mommy and Daddy gave in to temptation and had a torrid, secret affair and lied to everyone.*

Adam's phone beeped with a text message and he pulled it from his sweatshirt pocket. He smiled warmly at the screen. "My dad, congratulating me for the *Midnight Hour*."

The elevator dinged and the doors slid open.

"You were amazing," she said, stepping into the lobby as Adam held the elevator door. "I'm sure you'll get a lot of that today."

His phone beeped again. This time he didn't smile when he read the message. Instead, all blood drained from his face. "Hey, Carl," he yelled, panicked, across the lobby to the doorman. "Get Ms. Costello in a cab, right now."

"What's wrong?" She struggled to read his expression, her voice just as frantic as his when she had no idea what was going on.

"You have to go," Adam blurted, lurching for the elevator button. "My dad's on his way." The door slid closed.

Oh my God. No. The doorman rushed Melanie outside, but it was too late. She nearly ran straight into Roger Langford.

"Ms. Costello," Roger said. "Are you?" He peered through the glass door into the lobby of Adam's building. "Were you meeting with Adam?"

Melanie had never been so mortified in her entire life. "Uh, yes. Yes, sir." It felt awful to say it. "There was such a great response to Adam's interview last night. Just want to make the most of it. Make sure all of the media outlets are talking about it. Adam and I were just going over a few things." *Stop talking. Stop digging yourself a hole.*

"That's what I like about you, Ms. Costello. Always thinking, always working hard, never letting an opportunity pass you by."

Now she felt one million times worse. "Thank you, sir."

The doorman finally managed to flag a cab, signaling her with a wave.

Melanie was desperate to make her escape. "I should

go, sir. I need to get into the office." Technically not a lie, but getting through life on technicalities was no way to go.

"Sure, sure." Roger nodded. "Have a good day."

Adam paced in his kitchen. Had Melanie made it into a cab before his dad arrived? He had his answer as soon as his father stepped off the elevator into the apartment.

"I ran into Ms. Costello downstairs." His dad slowly unbuttoned his coat.

"Ah, yes," Adam replied, not wanting to offer any detail in case his story didn't match up with Melanie's. "Dad, please. Have a seat." He pulled out a bar stool just as he received a text. He glanced at his phone long enough to read Melanie's message.

We can't do this. It's not right.

He answered. Don't freak out.

"Hard worker, Ms. Costello." His dad slowly eased onto the high seat, his height making this a good spot for him to sit. "I only came by for a minute, Adam. I just wanted to tell you in person how happy I was with your appearance last night. I received several favorable phone calls from board members this morning. They were very impressed. I was very impressed. You were perfect."

Every word of praise from his father made Adam more conflicted. Now he understood firsthand exactly why Melanie was so uneasy. What if he told his father then and there that he and Melanie were involved? What would he say? Would he be disappointed? Accuse him of going back to his old ways?

The answer didn't matter. Melanie would be furious. If he stood any chance of keeping her, he couldn't jeopardize everything she'd worked so hard for.

If it was Adam's call and his professional butt was on

the line, he might be tempted to throw caution to the wind, risk every personal achievement and dollar in the bank to have the opportunity to be with Melanie like that, every night. It wasn't merely as good as he remembered. It was so much better.

By the time his dad was gone and Adam could reply to Melanie's text with something of substance, he wondered if he'd managed to calm her with his last message. He took care to be reassuring in case he hadn't.

Take a deep breath. Everything is fine. I'm coming to your office.

Her response was too quick for his liking.

Please don't. It will just make things worse.

He fired off a text to his assistant to move his morning meetings. He then turned his phone facedown on the kitchen counter. He wasn't about to get into an extended back-and-forth with Melanie via text message, like a couple of love-struck teenagers. He had to see her. Once he had her in his arms, everything would be fine.

He showered quickly and once downstairs, instructed his driver to get to Melanie's office as fast as possible. Every red light they sat at was torture. Adam's phone kept ringing, but he couldn't concentrate on work and finally had to silence it. Business would have to wait. Nothing was more important than seeing Melanie.

He practically leaped out of the car when they arrived at her office building. The elevator was out of service and he took the stairs two at a time up eight flights, all in a suit and tie. He pushed open the door at Costello PR, the office eerily quiet, except for the chime that announced the arrival of a visitor and his heavy breaths.

"Mel? Are you here?" He straightened his tie and jacket, striding through reception and back to the hallway leading to her office. He craned his neck around the corner. Her door was open. He heard sniffles. *Oh, no. She's crying.* He cleared his throat loudly, not wanting to frighten her. "Mel?"

She peeked out of her office, cheeks red and tear-stained, still as beautiful as could be. "Adam. I told you not to come. I don't want to talk about it. Just go away. We can't do this. I won't do this. It's not right."

"Mel, it was just a close call with my dad this morning. He doesn't know or suspect a thing. It's fine."

She ran her slender fingers through her blond hair, leaning her shoulder against the wall as if it was too difficult to stand. "That's so easy for you to say. You don't have as much to lose as I do. This isn't just my business or my profession. It's my whole life. My entire identity is tied to this stupid office I can't afford. My whole life revolves around keeping the lights on and moving forward. I have nothing else. I can't afford to make a mistake."

His heart twisted in his chest. How he hated that word— *mistake.* "And do you think last night was a mistake?"

"If I get fired from the most important job of my career, then yes."

His mind scrambled, unwilling to believe that she would really be that bad off if she got fired. There had to be a way around it. "What if I pay you the fee that he's promised you? Or let me buy your office space for you. Let me fix it if it all goes south." He stepped closer, longing to touch her, all the while sensing the impenetrable fortress she'd built around herself, and most important, her heart.

"Do you really think I want your money? That I want you to rescue me? I have to do these things for myself. I've been on my own since I was eighteen. I don't know any other way. And don't forget that the entire world knows

I've been working on this project. Every future client is going to ask me about it, they're going to want to know what Roger Langford had to say about the job I did. If he has to tell them that he fired me because I slept with his son, I'm destroyed. I'm done. There's no coming back from that."

"If I came back from my scandal, you could absolutely come back from that."

"Our situations aren't the same. You're Adam Langford. Your family represents the American dream and you're smart and handsome and a self-made man. The world *wants* to love you. I just had to show them the good in you. I'm nobody, Adam. If this comes out, I'll become a footnote, and I can't turn into that. I won't slink back to Virginia with my head held in shame and tell my dad that he was right, that I had no business moving to New York and thinking that I could run my own PR firm. I just don't think you understand the ramifications."

He did understand where she was coming from, but it didn't change the fact that standing here, even with her trying to claw her way away from him, he wanted her in his arms. He wanted her in his life. "I hear everything you're saying, but taking a chance on what's between us is more important than all of that. I think this is about more than your career or my family."

The look that fell on her face was one of utter confusion. "I don't know what you're talking about. There is nothing else."

He dared to inch closer, grasp her elbow. The instant he touched her, he felt exactly how much she'd closed herself off from him. "Think about what set you on this path. Your ex. He's the reason you're in this situation with your finances and your career, but I think he's also the reason you're so afraid to let somebody into your life."

Her eyes swept back and forth across his face. "No.

You're wrong. It's been more than a year, and I've made it work without him."

He nodded in affirmation, seeing that she was struggling with this particular revelation. He knew how she felt. He'd given in to tunnel vision before, focusing on a single goal so hard that he'd forgotten what mattered. "I care about you, Mel. A lot. I understand what it means to be hurt. We've all been hurt. Maybe I haven't gone through exactly what you have, but I understand. I do. And I know that there could be something real between us if you'll just let me in." He gazed into her stormy blue eyes, which were clouded with bewilderment. She needed time. He could see it. As hard as it would be to give her time, he had to. "I want you to think about that. I really want you to think about what that means."

She straightened her stance, sucked in a deep breath. "This isn't just about what you want, Adam. This is about what I want, too."

"Then tell me what you want."

"Right now? I want you to leave and go on with your life and promise me you won't think about me at all once the gala is over."

It felt as though someone had a stranglehold on his heart. Those were not the words of a woman who was ready to think about everything he'd said, everything he'd put on the line. "I can promise a lot of things, but I can't promise that. Not after last night."

"Well, you're going to have to try because I have a job to do."

Sixteen

Friday marked five days without a word from Adam. At least not directly.

Most of his interviews were complete, but there were a few loose strings to be dealt with, and most important, they needed to polish the speech he would give at the gala. They had a back-and-forth about his remarks for Saturday night, but it had all been funneled through his assistant. However much it crushed her, she couldn't blame Adam for shutting her out like that. After all, she'd told him flat out to forget her.

The person Adam had apparently not shut out was Julia. The two of them quickly cropped up in the papers again, holding hands while shopping in SoHo, only two days after Melanie and Adam had made love. By now, the photographers had an uncanny ability to find Julia. Either Julia's publicist was feeding them information or Julia and Adam had figured out how to do it on their own. It certainly wasn't Melanie's doing.

In fact, the whole thing was Melanie's *undoing*. How did she end up right back in the same boat she'd been in weeks ago? Scrutinizing pictures in a newspaper like a crazy woman, looking for absolute confirmation that Adam and Julia were either real or fake. She hated that she was still asking these questions. She hated that she still cared, but she did. She cared so much that it felt as if everything inside her was dying.

The things Adam had said to her that morning in her office played on a continuous loop in her head. *There could be something real between us if you'll just let me in.* She wasn't convinced it was that simple. If anything, it was the impossible, masquerading as simple. Was Adam right? Had Josh damaged her so badly that she'd become incapable of trusting someone? Was her heart really that closed off? She didn't want to believe she'd become that way, but maybe she was used to it. And if she were that way, what would fix it? Therapy? Meditation? Leaping off the curb into the path of an oncoming bus?

Melanie took in a deep breath of resolve, stepping onto the elevator up to Adam's apartment. Today was the day they'd planned to go over his speech and discuss what he would wear for the gala tomorrow night. *You can do this. You'll be fine.* She didn't have much of a plan for dealing with Adam, beyond being professional. Adam, hopefully, would do the same. He'd run through the speech and show her what he planned to wear. She'd give him the thumbs-up and disappear. Then her only remaining hurdle would be the gala, and that involved an open bar, fully stocked with champagne—sweet, merciful champagne.

When the elevator doors slid open, Adam was getting up from one of the bar stools at his massive kitchen island. "You're late." The icy edge to his voice made her feel about two feet tall.

"I am?" Melanie consulted her watch. "It's three minutes after five. You're always late."

"We aren't talking about me, are we? I have things to do tonight."

She sighed. So that was how he'd play this. She didn't want to take the bait, but the way he'd run back to Julia really ate at her. "Hot date with America's sweetheart?"

"Would that make you feel better? If your suspicions proved true?"

Adam's words hurt, even when she couldn't blame him for being angry. She'd been awful to him the last time she'd seen him.

"Let's deal with your suit and the speech, please."

Melanie followed Adam as he stalked back to his bedroom. The instant she was through the doorway, it felt as if something punched a hole in her chest, right where her heart was. The bed caught her eye, pristinely dressed with silky white bedding. It took no effort to remember exactly what it felt like to be with him tangled up in those sheets, the two of them so perfectly in sync. There were no issues in bed. It was everything outside the bedroom that was complicated.

If she'd thought this through, she could've moved the wardrobe discussion and speech practice to a less-intimate venue. Too late.

"I picked out three suits if you want to weigh in on it," Adam said, apparently unbothered by the presence of the sumptuously appointed, pillow-soft horizontal surface between them. "I'm leaving the tie to you." He stepped into his walk-in closet, pointing to the valet hooks where the suits were waiting, as well as his vast selection of silk ties.

Melanie already knew she wanted him to wear the dark charcoal-gray suit. He'd worn it the night she first met him and he looked absolutely incredible in it—jacket perfectly tailored to accentuate his sculpted shoulders and trim waist. So she'd have to avert her eyes and bite down on her knuckle every time she saw him tomorrow night. No big deal. She'd endured worse.

She thumbed her way through his ties. The quiet in the closet was suffocating. She had to say something. "Why no tuxedos?"

Adam cast his eyes away when she looked at him. "My mother hates the way my dad looks in black. She says he looks like an undertaker, which, given the circumstances, is probably an image we want to avoid."

"Yes. Of course." *So much for small talk.* She selected a few ties—a steely blue, black with a deep green diagonal stripe, and lavender.

"No way." Adam plucked the light purple tie from her hand and hung it back up. "You and your lavender. It's too girlish."

"It's your tie. Why do you have it if you can't even stand to look at it?"

"It was a gift from my mother. I think of her every time I choose not to wear it."

She deliberated between the other two ties before thrusting one into his hand. "Fine. We'll try the blue. It'll bring out your eyes."

"You care about how my eyes look. Really?"

"Yes, I care. Your eyes are one of your best features."

"If I didn't know better, I'd say you were flirting with me." He twisted his lips. "But I definitely know better."

"Just put on the suit so you can run through your speech and we can both get on with our night. I'll be outside the door."

He let out a frustrated grumble. "Okay. It'll just take me a minute."

Melanie wandered out of the closet and over to the window, looking out at the city. The days were getting longer, only a few months until summer. Where would she be by then? Would she have a few more clients? More money coming in? Logic said that she was on an upward trajectory, thanks to the success of Adam's campaign. So why wasn't she happy? She'd made the choice to focus on her career and it was going to pay off, but it all felt empty. She had no one to share these triumphs with, and as Adam had suggested, that was likely her own doing.

Adam strolled into the room, stopping in front of the full-length mirror on the wall. "Thoughts?"

Melanie steadied herself, leaning against the window casing. He was so handsome, it hurt to take a breath, producing a sharp pain in her chest. Her exhale came out as an embarrassingly choppy rush of air.

"That will work." She straightened, trying to play it off as a triviality when all she felt was a profound tingle from head to toe. Not getting to kiss him while he was wearing that suit was torture. Even worse was knowing that she wouldn't get to watch him take it off.

"What are you wearing to the party?" he asked.

"A dress."

"I assumed as much. Care to elaborate?"

"I don't know." She *hadn't* figured it out and it wasn't in the budget to buy anything new. She'd probably just go with one of her reliable little black dresses she'd worn to this sort of event hundreds of times. "Why does it matter?"

"I'm curious." Adam adjusted the cuff on his shirt. "Are you bringing a date?" His eyes didn't stray from his reflection in the mirror.

Melanie closed her eyes for a moment. This was supposed to be her chance to level the playing field tomorrow night, but she was now far less enthusiastic about the prospect. "I'm going with my neighbor, Owen. He's a doctor." She had zero romantic interest in Owen, and she'd made it clear this was just as friends, but Adam didn't need to know that. She simply refused to attend the party without a date, knowing that she'd have to smile and pretend to be happy while Julia was on Adam's arm.

"Let me guess. Ear, nose and throat."

"Gynecologist, if you must know."

Adam laughed. "You can't be serious."

"Why would I joke about that? Especially knowing what you'd probably say?"

"This is your event. I take it that you asked him out?"

What is he implying? That I can't get a date? "I invited him, but Owen has asked me out plenty of times."

"And have you gone? Out with Owen?"

"We've gone to the movies and out to dinner." She stopped short of clarifying the true context of the outings. They were not dates. There was popcorn and sitting together in the dark, but there was no hand-holding. There was dinner, but it was a slice of pizza at the Famous Ray's near their building. No romance, just friends, at Melanie's request.

"I see. Well, I look forward to meeting your doctor neighbor. I'm sure we'll have a lot to talk about."

"Because you're both so familiar with the female form?"

He delivered a look that shot ribbons of electricity through her body. "We're both big fans of Melanie Costello's form, apparently."

His words ushered in waves of heat, followed by a rush of confusion. Was he jealous? She couldn't imagine Adam envying another man. But what about the look in his eyes and the possessive rumble of his voice? Was he saying that he hadn't given up? And what would she do about that if it were the truth?

"You should probably practice your speech, so I can hear it out loud," she said, breaking the spell of silence.

"Right here?"

Melanie shrugged. "Sure." She trekked across the room to sit, even though she'd been inches from the bed, a perfectly acceptable perch if she hadn't been so afraid of what Adam might think.

"I almost wish I had a podium. Feels strange to stand here and deliver a speech." He straightened his jacket, seeming both confident and vulnerable standing before her. She stifled a sigh. That was the Adam she adored, the Adam who would never be hers.

Adam started his speech, but Melanie noticed something wrong right away. Everything that came out of his mouth was confident and optimistic, but his shoulders had tensed, his voice held a distinct edge of agitation. It was as if he was speaking someone else's words, but he'd written most of the speech. She'd made only a few minor changes and suggestions.

I'm excited for this new challenge.

I've been waiting my entire life for this opportunity.

I appreciate the confidence of the board of directors.

He was saying one thing while meaning another, which couldn't be good. After all, Adam had told her countless times. He was no good at faking anything.

Adam pinched the bridge of his nose when he finished his speech. He didn't even want to hear Melanie's appraisal. He'd seen the bewildered look on her face when he spoke.

"Everything okay?" she asked.

"Um. Sure." Her question caught him off guard to say the least. She didn't shy away from criticism when warranted, and he knew he hadn't done well. "Why?"

"It just didn't seem like you. At all."

"I'm fine." The words sat on his lips—nothing was fine. Everything was very much not okay, and it was about more than LangTel. It was more than worry about his dad. It was about her. The two of them in his apartment, being barely civil and making a grand point to not touch each other, hell, trying to not *look* too much at each other, was utterly and completely wrong.

But things had changed. Every other time she'd said no to him, it had been because they were working together. It was never because there was another man in the picture. The more egotistical parts of him had presumed that there was no other love interest because she wanted to be with him. Apparently he was wrong.

Now she had a date, a man she'd chosen, a doctor, no less. Adam never compared himself with other men, but this was pretty clear-cut. She'd shut down Adam three times. She'd chosen Owen. Maybe she wasn't closed off to the idea of love. Perhaps she was closed off only to the idea of him.

"Are you sure?" Melanie asked. "You seem like something's bothering you. Tell me what's going on."

Here she was, right before him, the woman he couldn't chase out of his mind if he wanted to. She wanted to listen. She wanted to talk. This could very well be their last chance to be together like this, just talking. After the gala, he would go his way and she would go hers.

He sucked in a deep breath and blew it out slowly. "I don't want to run LangTel." Just getting that much off his chest was a relief of epic proportions.

Melanie's mouth went slack. "What? But your dad. The succession plan." She looked around the room, blinking as if she couldn't comprehend what he'd said, which was a big part of the problem. It only made sense to Adam and Anna. Nobody else seemed to get it. "You love a challenge and it's a huge corporation, your family's name is on it. Why wouldn't you want that opportunity?"

He shook his head, dropping to the bench at the foot of his bed. "I know it sounds crazy, but every Langford man before me has been a self-made man. My dad. My grandfather. My great-grandfather. I can't stand the thought of not doing the same thing, blazing my own trail. I want something that I built myself, from the ground up. Is that so wrong?"

She smirked. "Adam, you said it yourself. You made your first million out of your dorm room. You're already a self-made man. Check that off your list and move on to the next big challenge. I have no doubt that you'll kick some serious butt running LangTel. With your mind for technology, you could do some incredibly innovative things."

"You're sweet, but it's not quite as simple as that. At least not for me it isn't."

"But haven't you and your dad been talking about this since you were a little boy?"

Indeed, Adam had been made keenly aware of what had been preordained for him. One of his most vivid childhood memories was of the day his dad brought him into LangTel on a Saturday afternoon, sat him down in the big leather executive chair in his father's corner office. Adam was seven. His dad had talked about things Adam didn't fully understand, told him that the chair and the desk and the whole damn thing would be his one day.

That day was fast approaching and Adam wanted nothing more than to slam on the brakes and make this runaway train come to a complete stop. The future his dad wanted for him wasn't what he wanted for himself.

"Yes, people have been talking about it since I can remember. In the end, I just can't say no to him, especially now that he's dying. If I'd been smart, I'd have said something about this years ago. I just didn't think I'd be confronted with it until he was ready to retire, and I always figured there was a chance I might feel differently by then."

Melanie's eyes grew wide. She hopped forward to the edge of her seat. "But Anna. She wants to do it. She told me when we met about planning the gala. Adam, that's it. It's perfect."

Adam smiled wide. She was so adorable, wanting to help, wanting to fix things for him and for his sister. Hell, she wanted to fix things for the entire Langford family. "Our dad refuses to entertain the subject. He's so old-fashioned, it's ridiculous."

Melanie appeared crestfallen. "Damn. I figured sibling rivalry was the bigger issue." She sighed deeply, their eyes connected, and he sank into them as if they were the only respite he would ever want. "Oh my God, Adam. The scandal. That was your out." She rubbed her temple, seeming even more concerned than she'd been a minute ago. "You could've said no to the PR campaign and just let the board of directors force you out. It would've solved everything."

He almost wanted to laugh. He'd considered that, but then his dad had hired a public relations whiz named Melanie Costello. The moment he saw her picture on her company's website, his heart had wormed its way into his throat. He finally knew the identity of his Cinderella. So he'd sucked it up and agreed to the PR campaign, even though it would likely seal his fate. He had to see his mystery woman again, see if the lightning in a bottle was real. And it was. It just wasn't meant to last.

He couldn't tell her that now—she'd moved on. He had no choice but to accept it. "I thought about that. But it would've made a mess of the family name, and that would have been no way to say goodbye my dad. It really wouldn't have solved everything, but it might have fixed that one problem." He couldn't have lived with himself if he'd taken that route anyway. It would've destroyed his relationship with his dad. Luckily, Melanie had saved him from making that choice. She just didn't know it.

"You know, the day I met with Anna, I felt a little jealous of your family," Melanie said.

"It's not all wine and roses, believe me."

"I know that, but you're still close, you really care about each other. I just don't have that. My sisters think I'm an oddball, my dad is impossible, and my mom is— Well, I never really knew her." She shook her head. "I know your relationship with your dad is tumultuous, but at least you have him. He's still here. You can still talk to him. You just have to find a way to get him to understand. You won't feel right about things if he passes away and you haven't tried one more time."

He'd tried and failed at it more times in the past few months than he could remember. Was that even possible? "How ironic is it that my dad and I are so close and he's the one person I never push to see my side of things? The idea of letting him down is still unfathomable."

Jack lumbered into the room, making a pit stop at Adam's knee, then beelining to Melanie. How that dog loved her. Adam toyed with telling Melanie that Jack had taken to standing next to the bed at night, resting his head on the pillow where she'd slept. Even Jack knew that she belonged there.

Melanie ruffled Jack's ears and smiled at him. "I'm no expert, but it's better to come out with things and live with the consequences. I did that with my dad. It didn't go over well, but at least I said my piece."

She was so smart, so intuitive about people, although she seemed more interested in helping others than examining her own problems. "I like hearing about your family." *It makes me feel closer to you.* He'd wanted to say that last part so badly, but it would sound too much as if he'd fallen desperately in love with a woman he couldn't have. And he had. He loved Melanie with every fiber of his being.

"I should probably go." She stood, straightening her dress and collecting her purse. "And you should get out of that suit so you don't get it all wrinkly before tomorrow."

He rose to his feet to say his goodbye, finding her only a few feet from him. His arms ached to hold her, never let go. He wanted to kiss her for days, escape from the entire world with her. He wanted to cherish and adore her the way she deserved to be. She'd shown him the opportunity in tomorrow, the day he'd been dreading, reminded him that he determined his own destiny. Of course, that pertained to business. There was no controlling it when it came to love, now that there was another man in the picture.

Seventeen

Melanie had rendered herself dateless right after she left Adam's. As difficult as it would be to see him with Julia at the gala, taking Owen as her human security blanket wasn't right. So, she stopped by his apartment, apologized profusely and owned up to everything. He deserved better and she needed to get her head screwed on straight.

She hardly slept at all that night, haunted by images of Adam, the way he'd looked at her after he'd tried on the suit, the gravel in his voice when it seemed as if he might be jealous. Other memories swooped in and out of her consciousness—the mountain house, dancing at Flaherty's, the night when she'd finally allowed herself the pleasure of the sexiest man she'd ever known. She could still feel his tender lips on hers, remember his warm and welcoming smell, conjure the safe sensation of his arms around her. Knowing that her chance with Adam was behind her left a void—one that made the one left by Josh look like a chip on a china teacup.

In the morning, sleep-deprived and feeling duly horrible, she knew she had to keep herself busy on gala day or it'd mean hours of rehashing what she'd gone over countless times. She was going to miss the hell out of Adam and there was no getting around it. She tried on twenty different dresses, threw in a load of laundry, smeared on a facial mask, took a bath, painted her nails ruby red, and spent entirely too much time messing with her hair and makeup. At least she would look good when she said goodbye.

Just when she'd narrowed her choice of dresses down to two, a push notification arrived on her phone. She picked it up and checked it—big mistake. It felt as though her breath was being dragged out of her as she looked at the tabloid photo of Julia leaving Adam's apartment building early that morning. So that was what Adam had on his social schedule last night. Julia had been on her way over.

She plopped down on her bed, still in her bathrobe. She stared at the picture, struggling to make sense of the emotion seething inside her. Logic said that this should make her sad, another sign from the universe that she and Adam weren't meant to be. But there was no melancholy. She didn't even feel bitter. She was flat-out pissed off—not at Adam, but at herself. The most incredible man she'd ever met, the only man she wanted, was about to walk away and she was going to let him. Everything holding her back would expire at midnight, and then where would she be? A few bucks ahead and brokenhearted, that's where.

Julia wasn't what he wanted. She knew it. Even if he hadn't told her as much, her heart still knew better than to accept that. Her heart knew exactly the way it felt when she and Adam were together—complete, fulfilled, as if it didn't make sense to be anywhere else. And when they were apart, she was lost, not just without a map or compass, but without a destination.

In the moments when Melanie had been able to see past

the obstacles between herself and Adam, their chemistry was more real than anything she'd dreamed possible. The rest of the time, even when they were at odds, she'd been unable to deny his pull on her. She'd only learned to pretend it wasn't there.

She couldn't pretend anymore. She couldn't let him go. That would mean giving in to circumstances, and she didn't do that. She fought her way out of everything. She fought to survive after Josh left, but she'd never fought *for* him. He didn't deserve that much. But Adam wasn't Josh. Adam valued her drive and determination. He was caring and thoughtful. He wanted to see her succeed. More than that, he could set her on fire with a single look, and no other man had that effect on her. Adam was worth fighting for, even if he might say that she'd hurt him too many times. She would fight for the man she couldn't allow to walk away. It was time to start listening to her heart again.

Melanie tapped out a text to Adam.

Can we talk before the party? In person. Alone.

Her pulse thumped wildly in her throat. Everything she wanted to say was bottled up inside her. She merely had to let it out. But was she too late?

The instant she sent the message, her phone rang, Adam popping up on caller ID. "That was quick," she muttered to herself. "Hey. I just sent you a text."

"It just came through," he said. "That's funny."

Her heart thundered. "Funny?"

"The timing. I'm standing outside your building. Can you buzz me up? The intercom isn't working."

Outside my building? But why? Panic coursed through her. Her apartment was a mess and her room looked as if a tornado had leveled a department store—dresses and shoes everywhere. "I'm not even dressed."

"Doesn't matter. I need to talk to you."

With no time for straightening up or putting on clothes, much less thinking, she rushed out of her bedroom, pressed the buzzer, unlatched the chain and opened her door.

She stepped out into the hall and watched as he ascended the stairs. He made it nearly impossible to breathe. He was temptation on two legs, in a perfect-fitting suit and five o'clock shadow. Deliberating over whether the front or the back was his best side had been so stupid. The sum total of Adam was the best. "Is something wrong?"

"You might say that. I'm sorry I didn't call. I was worried you might not let me come over." He stood inches away, still making her feel as if she couldn't breathe. "I love the dress. Not quite what I pictured, but I appreciate the cleavage."

Melanie looked down. Her silk robe gaped in the front. Heat flooded her face, and she quickly covered up, inviting him in. "What's wrong? Is there a problem with tonight?"

"I could ask you the same thing. Why did you need to talk to me before the party?"

Now that she was confronted with him—his endlessly magnetic being—it was difficult to start. She only knew that she had to. "I saw the photo in the paper. I don't care if Julia spent the night at your apartment. I don't believe that you want to be with her."

He nodded carefully, killing her with every second of silence. "I'm glad you finally believe me. I came over to tell you that she won't be at the gala tonight."

Wait. Her brain sputtered. Was this just about work? "What?"

"Don't freak out. I know you've worked hard on the party, but I couldn't pretend anymore. That was the reason for the photos of her outside my apartment. Her publicist is fabricating a breakup, at my request. I had to put an end to it now. Not just for my sake. For your sake, too."

Was this him just being fed up with the charade? Or was there more? "I broke my date with the doctor. It wasn't right to take him."

"And why is that exactly?"

She held her breath, a deluge of thoughts crowding her consciousness. He deserved to know how she felt, the mile-long list of reasons she needed him. "Because I'm in love with you. And I don't want to be with some other man, even for a minute. I don't want to watch you walk away tonight." She erased the physical divide between them with a few steps. Just feeling the rhythm of his breaths calmed her, even when she wasn't sure how he felt about what she was saying. The expression on his face was one of shock, but was it horror? "You're my only thought before I go to sleep. You're the first thing I think about when I wake up. When something happens in my day, good or bad, I have this undeniable urge to call you and tell you about it. The only reason I don't do it is because of my job. But I need more than my career. I need you." Their eyes connected and she saw her first sign that he might be on board—he smiled.

"You do?"

"I do. And you were right. I let everything that happened with my ex turn me into somebody who doesn't allow herself to feel. I don't want to be that person anymore. It's making me miserable."

"I hate the thought of you unhappy." He nodded, taking her hand and rubbing it with his thumb. "I had to talk to you before the party because I didn't want you to disappear tonight like Cinderella. I had to see the look on your face when I finally said I love you." He shook his head in admonishment, but he was fighting a smile. "Of course you had to beat me to it."

Melanie's heart back-flipped, making her pulse kick into hyperdrive. "I'm sorry. It's just that I've hurt you so many times, I thought you deserved the truth, even when I wasn't sure what you'd say."

He cracked his half smile, the one that made her feel as if her heart was an ice-cream cone in the summer sun. He reached for her other hand. "I love you and I want to be with you, but I need to know that you're in this for real, for the long haul. I can't handle it if you get skittish and run off again."

A single tear rolled down her cheek. The man who'd once had a revolving cast of women wanted to know if *she* was capable of sticking around. "I only ever ran because I was scared of how badly it would hurt if it didn't work. I'm not scared anymore."

"I mean it, Melanie. The long haul." He reached into his jacket pocket and pulled out a small, navy blue box. "I want you to be my wife. I want to spend my life with you."

Melanie's hand flew to her mouth. She knew that box—it was from Harry Winston. She gasped when he opened it and revealed a stunning emerald-cut platinum engagement ring. She was almost scared to touch it, worried it might disappear—she'd only dared to fantasize about a moment like this with Adam. She'd never dreamed it might actually be true. "It's so beautiful."

"Do you want to try it on?"

She nodded eagerly.

He plucked it from the box and slid it onto her finger. The diamond sparkled like an entire constellation.

"Oh my God, Adam. I love it. But how'd you get a Harry Winston ring so quickly?"

"I made it worth their while to tend to my needs. And I believe there's a bigger question on the table at the moment."

She stopped staring at her hand, instead looking into the face she hoped she could wake up to every morning, forever. "You want to get married?"

"I figured that a signed document was the way to go with you." He grinned from ear to ear. "I'm hedging my bets here."

A breathy laugh escaped her. Was this really happening? Her entire future had done a one-eighty in a matter of minutes. "I never want to let you go. I want nothing more than to be your wife."

He tugged her to him possessively. "Come here." He wrapped one arm firmly around her waist, swept her bangs from her forehead with his free hand. "I can't believe you said yes to something. No argument or negotiation or anything."

She loved it when he took charge, held her in a way that said she was his. "Not just a little something either. A big something."

He cupped the side of her face, rubbed her jaw with his thumb, sending goose bumps across her chest, over her shoulders and down her arms. Then he kissed her— soft and heavenly, practically begging for her to lean into him. She threaded her arms inside his jacket, craving his warmth and touch. Every second of holding on to this incredible man washed away the misery of the past year. Adam was hers.

Now that Melanie was his, kissing her, having her in his arms, was so much more satisfying than Adam could've imagined. Pulled against his body, her heat radiated into him, spiking his body temperature. The suit wasn't helping. Her mouth was sweet, her tongue swirling in a deliciously naughty way, every second of it driving him insane. She was at least partially undressed beneath her robe. He'd seen the gorgeous swell of her breasts when he'd arrived at her door.

He pulled the tie at her waist, unwrapping the most precious gift he'd ever have, pushing the silky fabric from her shoulders to the floor. His hands slid down her back, cupping and squeezing the velvety skin of her bottom. *No panties. Perfect.*

Melanie laughed, her lips vibrating against his. It was so damned sexy. "Adam, honey, there's no time. We're supposed to be at the party by six thirty."

Her arms weren't merely buried inside his jacket. She'd dipped one of her hands below the waistband of his pants. It only made him that much more determined to have her, body and soul. Now.

"There's no way that you say you'll marry me and I don't take off your clothes and make you lose all sense of direction." He nuzzled her neck, taking in her intoxicatingly sweet fragrance.

"My hair. My makeup."

"I've seen your bed head. It's perfect."

She scoffed, but the look on her face, the flush of pure pink blanketing her cheeks, said she wanted him as badly as he wanted her. "I still need to figure out what I'm wearing. We have like twenty minutes. Tops."

"I'm at my best under pressure."

She reached down and palmed the front of his trousers, biting her lip. "So I feel."

He growled into her ear, nipped at her lobe. Her touch made him feel as if he might not last twenty seconds if he wasn't careful. The lower half of his body was buzzing with the prospect of claiming her. "Either we do it in the hall, or you take me back to your bedroom."

She grabbed his hand and rushed down the corridor. He loved watching her move like that—feminine curves in hurried motion. Even better, he eyed her beautiful bottom as he removed his jacket, tie and shirt while she gathered a pile of clothes from her bed and tossed them onto a chair. He stepped behind her as she threw back the quilt. She turned. Her bare breasts brushed his chest.

"Pants. You're still wearing pants." Melanie unbuckled his belt, unbuttoned his trousers. "Be careful. There's no time for ironing."

He fished the condom from his pocket, handed it to her and slung his pants over the footboard of her bed. He stepped out of his boxers.

Melanie raised an eyebrow and perched on the bed as she tore open the foil pouch. "Do you always walk around with a condom?"

"I brought a ring, Buttermilk. Of course I brought one."

He sucked in a sharp breath when she held him in her slender fingers and rolled on the condom. He kissed her, tasting her sweetness, lowering her down onto the bed. He stretched out next to her, pressing his lips to her shoulder, the graceful contour of her clavicle. Her skin tightened when he flicked her nipple with his tongue. He reached between her legs, moved his fingers in a steady circle at her center. She moaned in appreciation. He dipped lower with his hand, finding her more ready than he could have hoped for.

"Make love to me, Adam," she muttered. "I need to feel you."

It wasn't just their schedule that had him eager to oblige. The lusty purr of her voice fueled the blood flow between his legs. He'd never felt so primed.

He settled between her legs, gazing at her wide blue eyes and sexy smile as he eased inside her. She was impossibly warm, her body responding to his with subtle squeezes. He grappled with the wealth of pleasure—her beauty, the way it felt to be inside her, the fact that they'd finally worked through their problems—it would've been so easy to surrender to the physical sensations and close his eyes, but he couldn't stop looking at her. He'd waited too long.

She locked her legs around him. He wanted to take his

time, but there was so little, and he already sensed that she needed more. She arched her back, lifting her hips to meet him. Her head rolled to the side, her eyes closed. Her supple lips went slack, breaths becoming shallow. He kissed her neck, thrusting deeper, wanting her to know every inch of him. He knew her peak was about to rattle them both—she was already gathering around him in strong, steady pulses. She dug her fingers into his back, her breaths short and fast.

His entire body was as taut as a rubber band stretched to its limit. Her internal muscles continued to squeeze him, faster now. The instant she let go, he gave in to it, too. Swells of bliss crashed over him—again and again, subtly fading into contentment. He collapsed at her side, breathing heavily. She curled into him and peppered his face with sweet, delicate kisses.

"That was amazing, but I can't wait until after the gala when we can just do that all night long," he said.

"And don't forget that tomorrow is Sunday. We don't have to get dressed at all tomorrow if we don't want to."

He clasped a hand behind her neck and kissed the top of her head. "I love your beautiful brain."

"And I love you."

Better words had never been spoken. "I love you."

Melanie popped up onto her elbow, glancing over her shoulder at the clock. "I hate to say this, but we need to bust a move. The car will be here to pick me up in fifteen minutes." She pecked him quickly on the lips, then hopped off the bed and began rifling through the clothes she'd dumped on the chair.

He plucked his boxers from the floor, thinking about what she'd said—her car. His limo and driver were still downstairs waiting. Practicality aside, going to the party separately was ridiculous when he'd had his fill of absurdity over the past few weeks. "You taking a separate car makes no sense."

Melanie stepped into a silky black dress while he put on his pants and shirt. "Sure it does. We'll both be single tonight and when you're ready, we'll tell your parents. If you want, we can argue at the party. Just to make it realistic." She held the top of her dress to her chest, turning her back to him. "Can you help me with this?"

He tied the bow of her open-back dress. Not knowing what she'd say to the proposal, he hadn't thought out logistics before he'd come to her apartment. Tonight was going to be difficult enough. He couldn't stomach the thought of more pretending. "No way. We're going to the party together. As a couple."

Melanie whipped around, her eyes ablaze with their usual panic when she didn't like one of his ideas. "Adam, no. That's insane. The entire world is expecting you to get out of a limo with Julia tonight. It's bad enough that she isn't going to be there. It'll be ten times more scandalous if I'm on your arm."

"I don't care." He buttoned his shirt and tucked it in. "I don't want to wait anymore. I won't wait. I love you and you love me, and if that's not good enough for the rest of the world, then too bad."

She stepped into a pair of black heels. God he loved her legs. He couldn't wait for tonight when they could be wrapped around him again.

"It's very easy for you to have a cavalier attitude," she said, putting on earrings. "Your dad isn't going to rip your head off first. He'll rip off mine."

Adam shook his head. "I won't let him do anything of the sort. This is all on me. You held up your end of the deal."

"That's sweet, but you didn't sign a contract. I did." She hurried over to the mirror above her bureau and checked her hair, then began chucking cosmetics into a small black handbag.

He came up behind her and clutched her shoulders, making eye contact with her in the mirror. This was the first time he'd seen them together, as a couple. It was all he ever needed to see. "Enough pretending and worrying about what everyone else thinks. It all ends tonight."

Eighteen

Melanie had done some daring things in her life, but this might top them all. On what was possibly the biggest night of either of their careers, she and Adam were about to out themselves as a couple in front of the media and his family. Daring or not, love made it seem like a perfectly acceptable risk.

A hailstorm of camera flashes broke out the instant Adam's driver opened the limo door, followed by a deluge of shouting voices.

"Julia. Adam. Over here."

Of course, Melanie wasn't the woman they were expecting. She followed Adam out of the car, embarrassment threatening to envelop her, but she refused to do anything but hold her head high. Adam had been dead serious about it at her apartment. They'd allowed everyone else's expectations to get in the way of their love, and there would be no more of that. She could do this. She *had* to do this if she wanted to be with Adam, and she wanted that more than anything.

An audible gasp rang out from the crowd as Melanie stepped onto the red carpet. Again, an assault of shouts rang out.

"Adam. Who are you with?"

"Where's Julia?"

Adam firmly squeezed her hand, reminding her that he was there for her to lean on if needed. She half expected him to rush her up the red carpet and past the press, but he didn't. He led her ahead several steps and stopped, collected as could be. "Calm down, everybody. I'd like to introduce you all to Melanie Costello. She's in charge of my public relations."

"Where's Julia?"

That question had played a central role in Melanie's imagined worst-case scenario. The camera flashes became sporadic. The roar of the crowd dulled.

"You'll have to ask her that. We're no longer together, but it was an amicable split."

The litany of flashing lights returned to full speed, but Melanie didn't shy away. She was too busy beaming at her future husband. Adam had learned to deal with the media beautifully.

"Is Melanie your new girlfriend?" a female photographer asked.

"Let's just say that an announcement will be made later this evening." Adam leaned over and placed a kiss on her temple.

Melanie couldn't believe this was really happening. It was all like a dream when being with Adam was already surreal. She'd spent a year wishing she hadn't been so stupid as to sneak out of his apartment, and the past month wishing he could be hers. And now he was.

Melanie and Adam resumed their march up the red

carpet as other guests arrived behind them. The crowd ahead thinned, making it clear their course was about to bring them face-to-face with Roger and Evelyn Langford.

Adam pulled her closer, whispering in her ear, "It's okay. Let me do the talking. For once."

Melanie smiled, but her stomach was a restless sea. Roger could say anything he wanted in front of a ballroom of the wealthy and powerful. He could destroy her career with one well-worded sentence if he wanted to. Even though Melanie would eventually become Adam's wife, she wasn't about to throw away the company she had built. She would have what she'd once thought was unattainable—her career *and* Adam. Unless his father decided to make it all come crashing down.

"Dad. Mom," Adam said, when they reached the entrance to the grand ballroom.

Roger's jaw was set, as if he was biting down on a bullet. "We need to talk. Now." The anger in his voice was thinly disguised by a smile.

"You're right. We need to talk." Adam looked around the room. There were an awful lot of eyes on them. "Privately."

"There's a smaller ballroom next to this one." Melanie pointed to the near corner of the room. "It's empty. The hotel had said we could use it tonight if needed."

She led the way, her hand firmly held in Adam's, her heart pounding away in her throat. The entire crowd whispered as they walked past. She was keenly aware of Mr. and Mrs. Langford behind them, fearing what they must be thinking. This was not the way she wanted this meeting with her future in-laws to happen.

As soon as the door was closed behind them, Roger set his sights on Melanie. "You signed a contract." He pointed to Melanie's and Adam's joined hands. "And you've very clearly violated it. That morning I went by Adam's apartment. You weren't just dropping by to discuss work with Adam. You were there because you'd spent the night." Roger shook his head in dismay. "Poor Julia. She had no idea my son would break her heart."

Adam didn't let go of Melanie's hand, bringing her along as he moved closer to his father. "Dad, please don't speak to Melanie like that. And besides, it isn't good for you to get so riled up. Take a deep breath and listen to me." Adam's voice was calm and measured, but there was no mistaking his determination.

Evelyn Langford, in a midnight blue cocktail dress and lavish diamond necklace, gripped her husband's arm. "Darling. At least allow Adam to explain."

Roger folded his arms across his chest. "Come out with it then. And it'd better be good."

Adam's shoulders rose as he took a deep breath. "Dad, the Julia thing was a ruse and you knew it, but you refused to believe me. I was never anything less than completely honest with you about it." He squeezed Melanie's hand.

Adam's father appeared crestfallen, but Evelyn nodded in agreement. "You have to understand, Adam. Your father became very attached to the idea of you finding a wife and doing so while he was still here to see it."

Anna swept into the room, decked out in a black strapless dress. "There you are. Everyone's wondering where you went."

"We were discussing the things your brother has decided to do to make tonight more stressful," Roger said.

Adam kept a firm grip on Melanie's hand. "I take full responsibility if there's any fallout from tonight, but if that's the price of being with Melanie, then that's the price I'll pay. I love her too much to hide it anymore."

Anna's eyes lit up. "I had a feeling something was going on."

"You knew?" Roger asked.

Anna shrugged. "I had a hunch after spending time with Melanie. I could just tell from the way she talked about him. And it's not surprising that he'd be smitten. She's smart, beautiful and a great businesswoman."

It was such a relief to feel as though someone in the Langford family beyond Adam was in Melanie's corner.

"Dad, I love Melanie. I've asked her to be my wife and she said yes."

"You're getting married? After knowing each other for a month?" Roger's eyes were no longer filled with anger, but rather astonishment.

"You were excited to think I might marry Julia and it's not like she and I had much history."

"I suppose." Roger shook his head.

Adam turned back to Melanie. "Now what?" he mouthed.

Melanie took his elbow and pulled him close, delivering the message directly into his ear. "Speak from your heart. You hit a home run every time you do."

Adam kissed her on the cheek then faced his father again. "Dad, do you want to know the one thing in my life that I have never questioned? Not even once?"

"That you'd run LangTel someday?"

"No. That you and Mom loved each other. I can see it in the way you look at each other, hear it in your voices. I have that with Melanie. She understands me and cares about me. She'll be a real partner, and that's more than what I need. It's the only thing I want."

Melanie warmed from head to toe, unable to suppress her smile.

Evelyn cleared her throat. "Darling, do I have to remind you that you and I were engaged after two months?"

Roger had no answer for that, only a sigh.

"Love is love, Dad," Adam said. "I wasn't about to consult a calendar when I asked Melanie to marry me. The only thing I thought about was what my heart wanted."

"Don't forget that I was pregnant with Aiden when we got married," Evelyn said to Roger. "These things don't always look like a picture postcard. And it didn't matter that it happened that way. It didn't change the fact that we were a couple of kids, madly in love, and all we wanted was to be together."

Roger turned and looked at her sweetly. "I remember that day like it was yesterday. Best damn day of my life." The corners of his mouth turned up, but it was clear that she'd brought up something far more meaningful than a simple happy memory. It was about everything between them.

A tear rolled down Evelyn's cheek. "See? And you and I did just fine. Thirty-one incredible years of marriage. No one could ever want more than that."

"We did better than fine, Ev," Roger said. "It was perfect."

Now Melanie was fighting tears, witnessing for the first time the power of the love that bound Roger and Evelyn Langford. They were both so strong, so resolute, even when they knew very well they were about to lose each other forever.

"Dad, I just want you to be happy for me, be happy for us," Adam said. "Melanie's the most amazing woman I've ever met, and she's going to be part of this family."

"That's the most important thing, Dad," Anna said. "We need to welcome Melanie into our family. An engagement trumps whatever happens tonight."

"I know you want Adam to have love in his life and to get married," Evelyn said, her tears slowing. "And you've been singing Melanie's praises since the day you hired her. I don't really see what the problem is now that you know the truth." She turned quickly to Adam and Melanie. "Can we see about hurrying up the wedding so your father can be there for it?"

Adam's eyes connected with Melanie's and he cracked his half smile. They would have a lot to talk about once they were finally alone. "Sure," he said. "But there's one more thing Dad needs to hear."

Adam stepped closer to his father, resting his hand on his shoulder. Everything Melanie had said to him last night rang loud and clear in his head. His dad was still here. There was still time, and that meant it was time for the truth. "I can't run LangTel. I love you and you know I'll do anything for you, but I can't live your dream. More important, it's Anna's dream to run the company, and I can't sit by and watch her lose the chance."

His father didn't even feign surprise. He was at least aware of Adam's wishes, even if he'd dismissed them as ludicrous. "You really were serious about that."

"I should've forced the issue, but I wanted to make you happy. I love you, Dad, and I always want to make you proud." Adam couldn't remember the last time he'd cried, but after witnessing the powerful exchange between his parents and now seeing the look on his dad's face, his eyes misted. He embraced his father. There would be only so many more opportunities to do that. He didn't want to pass this one up. It was too precious. "LangTel will still be a family company if Anna runs it. We'll all still have the lives you want for us. She can still meet the perfect guy and get married."

Anna coughed. "Hey. No promises on finding the perfect guy."

Adam laughed, thankful his sister was willing to lighten the mood. "I'll be there whenever Anna needs me, but I have a feeling she won't need me at all. It really will work out. I know it will. I won't let anything go wrong. I promise."

His father sighed heavily. "I wish it were as simple as that. I can't pull a fast one on the board and give them a different succession plan. Even in my role as founder, I can't do that. You understand that as well as anyone, Adam."

Adam had to find a way to fix this, for Anna and for himself. "But I could do it myself, as CEO. The company bylaws leave the nomination to me. I looked it up."

"Well, sure, son, that's what I put in place, but you still need the approval of the board of directors. You know that."

"And that's what I'll do. Once things are stable and I have the full confidence of the board, I want to name Anna as CEO. It shouldn't take longer than a year." Adam knew full well the responsibility that scenario bore, but he had no choice. It was the only way for everyone to eventually get what they wanted. "I want your blessing to do that. I think Anna and I would both feel better knowing that you were okay with it."

"Yes," Anna said. "I need to know that you approve."

Roger looked back and forth between Adam and his sister for what felt like an excruciatingly long time. Whatever his dad had to say, Adam had the distinct impression that there would be no more discussion. This was it.

"You have my blessing," Roger said. "With everyone in this room as witness, you have my blessing."

Anna rushed ahead to hug Roger. Adam followed, embracing them both.

"Speaking of blessings," Evelyn interjected, "Melanie hasn't been welcomed properly, darling."

Melanie smiled sweetly as Evelyn hugged her, Roger watching the exchange. This was the moment Adam had envisioned for the two of them, now that she was going to be his wife and his father was accustomed to the idea.

"I'm sorry if we got off to a rough start this evening," Roger said as Evelyn took his hand again. "I apologize for that. I always liked you, Ms. Costello. You're smart and you know your stuff. I admire a woman who knows her stuff."

"Thank you, sir. I appreciate that."

"I'd like you to call me Roger, please. You've done your job and you've done it well, but you're no longer working for me."

Adam put his arm around Melanie. What a relief it was to hear his dad say that. No more contract. No more worrying about whether his dad might decide to crush her career.

"Please, call me Melanie."

Roger glanced at his wife. "Looks like we're going to get a Langford wedding after all, Evelyn. And as near as I can tell, a hell of a daughter-in-law."

"I'd say we're pretty lucky," Evelyn said, gazing up into Roger's eyes.

"We are indeed," Roger said. "And I'd love nothing more than to sit around and talk about it, but I'm afraid that there's a ballroom full of people waiting for me."

Adam nodded eagerly. "It's time."

They all made their way into the grand space, Adam's parents leading them, followed by Anna. Melanie and Adam, hand in hand, brought up the rear. Adam hadn't gotten *exactly* what he wanted with the LangTel situation, but he did have exactly what he wanted for the rest of his life—Melanie.

Roger took the stairs up to the podium slowly, Evelyn at his side. Melanie and Adam took their places at the head table with Anna. Before a roomful of hundreds of wealthy and powerful New Yorkers and a cavalcade of press, Adam's father began his speech.

"I want to thank everyone for joining us on what will be an important night in the history of LangTel. I'd like to formally announce that pending the board of directors' final approval, my son, Adam, will be taking the helm as CEO."

The crowd clapped enthusiastically.

"This changeover is going to happen as soon as possible," Roger continued. "Because I also must tell everyone that my doctors have declared my cancer terminal."

A marked hush fell on the room.

"But tonight is not about proclaiming a death sentence, it's about setting LangTel on a course for the future," Roger said, his voice booming in the space. "It is one of my final wishes that the board move Adam into this new role swiftly. Adam has demonstrated that he is an upstanding man and an excellent business leader. I couldn't be any more proud of him."

Melanie squeezed Adam's hand under the table. How different his father's proclamation would've sounded if Melanie hadn't convinced him to try one more time to change things, if he didn't have his father's blessing to let Anna take his place.

"I'd like to invite Adam up to the stage to make his remarks, and I believe he has some very happy news of a personal nature to share with everyone." Roger stepped away from the podium and embraced Evelyn.

Adam leaned over to Melanie, speaking loudly, so his voice could rise above the audience applause. "You're coming with me."

"Are you sure? It's your night."

"My parents are standing on that stage together. You and I are doing the same thing." He grabbed her hand and got up from the table, leading her up onto the stage. She stood with his parents as he took his place behind the podium.

Looking out at that sea of faces, he couldn't believe how different this moment was from the one he'd imagined. "I'll be quick because I know everyone would much rather dine on filet mignon than listen to me." The crowd laughed, setting Adam more at ease. "I'd like to thank my father for his confidence in me. I'm excited for this new

challenge and I won't let my father or LangTel down."
Now he could believe the words, unlike the time he'd prac-
ticed this speech for Melanie. With great joy, he tacked
on a sentiment that hadn't originally been in the speech.
"And as to the happy news my father mentioned, I'd like
to announce my engagement to Melanie Costello. We're
looking forward to planning a big Langford wedding and
spending our lives together." Everyone clapped and Adam
waved Melanie over, putting his hand around her waist.
"With that, I'd like to thank everyone for coming. Please,
enjoy the evening ahead."

Several board members were waiting for them once
Adam and Melanie stepped down from the stage. Either it
was the somber news of his father's prognosis, the fantastic job Melanie had done on the PR campaign, or renewed
confidence in Adam's abilities, but regardless, Adam received nothing but well-wishes from everyone he spoke
to. It was such a relief.

After dinner, Adam took Melanie's hand and led her to
a relatively quiet corner. "How long until we get to leave
and I get to peel that dress off you?" He was mentally exhausted, but he was sure he'd be able to muster all kinds
of energy once he had her alone and naked.

She rolled her eyes adorably. "I think we should stay
until midnight. Then we can go."

Adam's entire body warmed to the idea, and to the beautiful creature on his arm. "I'm guessing this was a little
more than you signed up for."

She laughed and straightened his tie. "This is a cake-
walk compared to my family. Believe me."

He took her hand, loving the feeling of the ring on her
finger, knowing that it meant their future together was
sealed. "The next year is going to be great, but it's also
going to be hell. We're probably going to lose my dad and

I'll be trying to convince the board of directors that another change in CEO is a good idea."

Melanie grinned sweetly. "And we have a wedding to plan, too. We'll get through it all. I know we will. Together."

"Tonight wouldn't have been possible without you. Seriously. And we've got to put Costello Public Relations on the map. You need an influx of cash so we can hire some staff for you. Let you focus on what you're so good at."

"And what is that exactly?"

"Your mastery of the world of public relations. You're the only person I know who could convince the world that I have a good side."

"I've seen you naked, Adam Langford." She nuzzled his neck, sending a jolt of electricity through his body. "Trust me, you have more than one good side."

* * * * *

If you loved this story of romance in the workplace,
pick up these other office romances from
Harlequin Desire!

AFTER HOURS WITH HER EX
by USA TODAY *bestselling author*
Maureen Child

THE BOSS'S MISTLETOE MANEUVERS
by Linda Thomas-Sundstrom

FOR HER SON'S SAKE
by USA TODAY *bestselling author*
Katherine Garbera

NOT THE BOSS'S BABY
by Sarah M. Anderson

HIS BY DESIGN
by Dani Wade

If you're on Twitter, tell us what you think of
Harlequin Desire! #harlequindesire

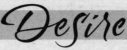

REQUEST YOUR FREE BOOKS!

2 FREE NOVELS PLUS 2 FREE GIFTS!

HARLEQUIN®

Desire

ALWAYS POWERFUL, PASSIONATE AND PROVOCATIVE

Isabella was somehow even more beautiful than he'd remembered. And probably more treacherous, Marc reminded himself as he fought for control.

It had been six years since he'd seen her.

Six years since he'd held her, kissed her, made love to her.

Six years since he'd kicked her out of his apartment and his life.

And still, he wanted her.

It came as something of a shock, considering he'd done his best not to think about her in the ensuing years.

All it had taken was a glimpse of her gorgeous red hair, her warm brown eyes, from the small window embedded in the classroom door to throw him right back into the seething, tumultuous heat that had characterized so much of their relationship. He hadn't cared about anything but getting into that room to see if his mind was playing tricks on him.

Six years ago he had kicked Isa Varin—now, apparently, Isabella Moreno—out of his life in the cruelest manner possible. He didn't regret making her leave—how could he when she'd betrayed him so completely?—but in the time since, he had regretted how he'd done it. When he'd come to his senses and sent his driver to find her and deliver her things, including her purse and cell phone and some money, she had vanished into thin air. He'd looked for her, but he'd never found her.

Now he knew why. The very passionate, very beautiful, very bewitching Isa Varin had ceased to exist. In her place was this buttoned-down professor, her voice and face as cool and sharp as any diamond his mines had ever produced. Only the hair—that glorious red hair—was the same. Isabella Moreno wore it in a tight braid down her back instead of in the wild curls favored by his Isa, but he would know the color anywhere.

Black cherries at midnight.

Wet garnets shining in the filtered light of a full moon.

And when her eyes had met his over the heads of her students, he'd felt a punch in his gut—in his groin—that couldn't be denied. Only Isa had ever made his body react so powerfully.

One look into her eyes used to bring him to his knees. But those days were long gone. Her betrayal had destroyed any faith he might have had in her. He'd been weak once, had fallen for the innocence she could project with a look, a touch, a whisper.

He wouldn't make that mistake again.

Will Marc have Isa back in his bed, trust be damned?

Find out in CLAIMED, the first of the DIAMOND TYCOONS duet by New York Times bestselling author Tracy Wolff, available wherever Harlequin® Desire books and ebooks are sold.

www.Harlequin.com

JUST CAN'T GET ENOUGH?

Join our social communities
and talk to us online.

You will have access to the latest
news on upcoming titles and special
promotions, but most importantly,
you can talk to other fans about your
favorite Harlequin reads.

Harlequin.com/Community

 Facebook.com/HarlequinBooks

Twitter.com/HarlequinBooks

Pinterest.com/HarlequinBooks

THE WORLD IS BETTER WITH Romance

Harlequin has everything from contemporary, passionate and heartwarming to suspenseful and inspirational stories.

Whatever your mood,
we have a romance just for you!

Connect with us to find your next great read,
special offers and more.

f /HarlequinBooks

🐦 @HarlequinBooks

www.HarlequinBlog.com

www.Harlequin.com/Newsletters

H HARLEQUIN®

A Romance FOR EVERY MOOD™

www.Harlequin.com